Braver with You

Jaycee Weaver

Sandia Sky Press

Table of Contents

Chapter One 1

Chapter Two..6

Chapter Three 10

Chapter Four 17

Chapter Five 23

Chapter Six 31

Chapter Seven 35

Chapter Eight 41

Chapter Nine 47

Chapter Ten... 51

Chapter Eleven..56

Chapter Twelve 60

Chapter Thirteen..67

Chapter One

Ashlyn Scott darted out of the boutique, glancing up and down the street before crossing to her car. If her mother knew what she was doing right now, she'd never hear the end of it. For years she'd cowed to the demands, the cajoling, the needling, the guilt trips, but not this time. She lifted the weighty garment bag off her shoulder and spread it across the back seat, making sure to tuck the edges safely inside.

The guilt didn't hit until she'd buckled her seat belt.

What had she done?

Stop, Ash, you did nothing wrong.

Then why did it feel as if she'd just stolen that dress? Why the urge to floor it from the scene of a crime?

Mom was why.

Or perhaps it was what this moment represented—a whole new trajectory apart from what had been planned for her life since she was five. A life she enjoyed, mostly, but was it so wrong to want it on her own terms for once?

Her brown eyes connected with her glasses-wearing reflection in the rearview mirror before flicking to the gleaming vinyl bag. A thrill raced through her at the monumental secret now in her possession. It would upset her mother, but right then, Ashlyn couldn't bring herself to care. In fact, the mere memory of how she'd looked not fifteen minutes ago, how she'd nearly broken

down in front of the poor sales lady because she'd found *the dress*—
with no one's help or involvement—emboldened Ashlyn's resolve.

It might have started with a dress, but it wouldn't end there.

Or maybe it would.

Ashlyn wavered. She *hated* being gutless and indecisive.

She started the car and braced against the blast of hot air,
sending up a prayer of thanks when it turned cold. Pressing a finger
to the Voice Dial button on the steering wheel, she called the one
person who'd support her unconditionally.

"Hey, babe." Conrad's voice filled her with peace. "How did it
go?"

"Amazing."

His soft chuckle brought a picture of his sideways smile to
mind. "Found what you were looking for?"

"I did." She let out a happy sigh. "I can't believe we're doing
this."

"I'm still not sure about the secrecy angle, but I understand
your reasoning."

Conrad was honest to a fault, and asking him to participate in
this deception would come at a cost. But after two decades of
suffocating under her mother's influence, this was the only way.

"Thank you." She checked her mirrors, still feeling like she was
getting away with the heist of the century. Silly, when she'd forked
over a hefty chunk of her paycheck for the symbol of her
independence. "When are you coming home?"

"Tomorrow afternoon."

"How did the interview go?"

He paused.

Ashlyn perked to attention, not an easy feat while driving sixty-
seven miles an hour on I-25 with as much adrenaline as she had
flowing through her veins.

"Aced it."

"Oh." She frowned. "Then what's the problem?"

"The job's in Cañon City, Colorado."

"Oh," she repeated.

"Yeah." His heavy exhale told her all she needed to know.

He wanted this job, but he worried about taking them away
from the safety and comfort of Albuquerque. She understood
better than anyone—both the desire to leave and the gut-

clenching fear while staring over the edge of the nest. Especially with their mother hens discouraging them from flying the coop.

It was time to be brave.

"Where you go, I go. We're a team, and I fully support your decision," she said with conviction.

"Are you sure?" Layers of meaning filled those three simple words.

Was she sure about moving? Yes. Sure about leaving their mothers behind? Also, yes. About marrying Conrad and following him wherever his job took them? A thousand times, yes.

"You know better than to ask me that."

She didn't need to see his smile to know he wore one. They'd been best friends as far back as either could remember and read each other's faces better than a beloved book.

"I do."

"Practicing the words already, are you?"

He answered with another light chuckle. "Counting the days."

Ashlyn's heart did a playful schoolgirl skip in her chest. Could this man be more perfect for her?

"Me too. T-minus forty-five days."

"Can't wait."

"Same. Love you. Enjoy the rest of your trip."

"You too."

The call disconnected as Ashlyn navigated the final turn and parked in her usual spot against the curb in front of her aunt's single-story adobe home in northeast Albuquerque. She closed her eyes and breathed in and out for several long beats before glancing at the garment bag on the back seat and scanning the area. Coast was clear.

Ashlyn hefted the bag over her shoulder and pushed the bridge of her glasses back into place before letting herself in with her spare key.

"Aunt Wendy?"

Silence. *Praise the Lord.*

Ashlyn wasn't ready to share the dress with anyone, not even the woman who'd staunchly supported every one of Ashlyn's mini-rebellions over the years. She hauled the gown into the bedroom at the end of the hall, decorated in soft earthy colors and jewel-toned accents. This retreat was more her style than the too-girly bedroom she still lived in at Mom's house four streets over.

Treating the bag like a fragile antique book, Ashlyn placed it on the bed and smoothed the edges to keep the contents from wrinkling while she cleared space in the closet.

She'd just finished moving the last of her wedding stash out of the way when she heard the garage door motor followed by the familiar jangle of her aunt's keys.

"Hey, kid! Adding to the pile?"

"Yes ma'am!" Ashlyn hesitated, hanger in hand. Aunt Wendy would see the dress eventually. What would it hurt to show her now?

What if she tells Mom?

Stop. Aunt Wendy, her father's sister, had been her champion every day of Ashlyn's nearly twenty-five years on earth. There was little love lost between her aunt and mother. Ashlyn fretted over nothing.

"Is it safe to come in?"

Relief brought a smile to Ashlyn's lips. "Yeah, come on in."

Wendy entered the bedroom wearing her yoga clothes and a mischievous grin.

"Missed you in class today."

"I know, but it was the only appointment available on my day off." She'd have to practice her own flow later tonight to soothe the tension between her shoulders if she wanted to sleep through the guilt.

"Ooh, you found your dress! Can I see?"

Ashlyn appreciated how Wendy left the decision up to her, without pressure. She debated giving in but keeping the dress to herself felt like the right move—for now. Chewing the inside of her cheek, she flashed an apologetic look and shook her head.

"Say no more, honey bunch." Wendy winked and waved to the closet. "Hide it in the back, and I promise not to peek."

Relief and gratitude surged through Ashlyn. This was why she trusted Aunt Wendy, why she'd come here instead of hiding the dress in her closet at home. If Wendy promised not to peek, she wouldn't, where Mom wouldn't hesitate.

"You're the best."

"Love you, sweet girl. You hungry?"

4

Wendy laughed at the answering growl from Ashlyn's stomach.

"I guess that's a yes. I'll be in the kitchen."

Her aunt closed the door behind her, leaving Ashlyn to fully breathe for the first time in hours. Was she a terrible daughter for doing this?

She pictured the constricting vintage ivory satin gown hanging from her bedroom door at home, with its gaudy embroidery, itchy crinoline underskirt, and a million buttons down the back. With a shudder, she unzipped the bag to peek at the glorious unadorned white silk and chiffon dress.

Conrad would love the way it draped and flowed over her figure. This dress was *her* to a T. She couldn't wait to see his first glimpse of her in it, certain he'd have that look in his eyes every bride hoped for—the one that said she was the most beautiful gift, a treasure he felt lucky to behold.

She might be a terrible daughter, but in forty-five days, she'd become one blessed wife.

Chapter Two

A fierce yawn racked Conrad Greer as he let himself into his apartment. He dropped his duffel beside the door and collapsed onto the couch, aching for a nap. A throw pillow at one end—courtesy of Ashlyn—propped his head, and his feet rested on the opposite end. He stared at the ceiling, allowing his mind to wander while he prayed for a second wave of energy.

Yesterday's interview had gone better than he'd let on. The Colorado company had been headhunting him the better part of a year, but until recently, he hadn't even considered taking a job out of state. Especially one in his father's neck of the woods, though he'd managed to avoid a visit this time around.

Ashlyn might say she was okay with moving, but when push came to shove, would she go? Mrs. Scott was a crafty lady, especially when it came to working over her daughter.

Things weren't as tense with his mom as they were with Ashlyn's. She might not like it, but Mom would understand.

He tried to give Mrs. Scott grace. He'd been there when Ashlyn had gone missing and almost died, after all. The ordeal had forever changed *his* life too. It was why he'd become a helicopter pilot and search-and-rescue volunteer.

Now, ten years of helo training in high altitude and mountainous terrain, along with his extensive SAR experience, made him a valuable asset. This opportunity to work in Colorado's part of the Rockies would be difficult to pass up, but he'd turn down the offer if Ashlyn changed her mind.

Where you go, I go. From the day their Sunday school teacher taught the story of Ruth, it'd been their phrase.

An inseparable duo despite their two-year age difference, he couldn't remember a time when it hadn't been the two of them against the world. Well, maybe those few gangly, hormonal years between elementary and high school. Those had been awkward years, but weren't they for everyone? He and Ash preferred to pretend they never happened.

Conrad adjusted his neck with a satisfying crack and sat up, scratching the stubble along his jaw. Ashlyn would be closing up the library soon, and he needed to shower before their date.

Thirty minutes later, he strode into the kitchen for a glass of water, his blond hair damp and face smooth. His favorite jeans were in the hamper, but he'd caught Ashlyn admiring him in this particular pair more than once. The memory curved his lips. She wore plenty of things that elicited similar reactions from him.

They probably ought to refrain from tempting each other so flirtatiously, especially as the wedding clock counted down. Committed to waiting for rings, the physical boundaries they'd established years ago had grown in temptation.

Probably for the best they planned to dine out tonight. After two days away, he missed her fiercely. For childhood neighbors who'd spent most of their lives in each other's pockets, two days might as well be two months. Did that make him soft? Who cared? Conrad was man enough to acknowledge his feelings.

Traffic was light the few blocks from his apartment to the popular diner. He parked his brand-new redesigned Ford Bronco next to Ashlyn's Ford Focus and smiled. They'd be a Ford family in a Toyota world when they moved to Colorado.

If Colorado's Your plan for us, Lord, show us Your will.

Conrad spotted Ashlyn through the diner window, her long brown ponytail swinging as she made her way to the hostess stand. Once inside, he swept his fiancée into a bear hug. She squealed and peppered his face with kisses, to the hostess's amusement.

Good to know Ashlyn had missed him too.

Grinning like an idiot, Conrad set her feet on solid ground, laced their fingers, and followed the hostess.

"Thanks, Jane," he said when she halted at their favorite booth in the back.

"You guys enjoy. Try to keep the making out to a minimum, though, will you?"

Ashlyn glanced away and pushed her glasses higher on her nose, attempting to hide the color splashed across her cheeks. The familiar tic widened his smile.

"If you weren't my little sister . . ." With an exaggerated frown, he wagged his finger playfully at Jane.

The young hostess rolled her eyes. "Sister in Christ doesn't count, you oaf."

"Yeah, yeah. Say hi to Miss Ada and Mr. Kent for me."

"Will do." Jane grinned and strode back to the hostess station.

He motioned Ashlyn to sit first. She kissed his cheek and dropped into the right side of the navy-blue vinyl booth.

"In my head, she's still in high school. Seems so long ago we were all in youth group together."

"Not that long ago for you." He sat across the table.

"If you say so."

"I do."

She beamed. "Still practicing, huh?"

He tossed her a wink and reached for the menu despite knowing what he wanted. It provided cover while he searched for a segue to the Colorado offer.

"Mrs. Bennett called about scheduling our premarital counseling."

Conrad peered over the top of his menu and smiled at the light in Ashlyn's brown eyes, as effervescent as the root beer he suddenly had a craving for.

"Which Mrs. Bennett?"

Her smile widened. "The elder, but we should talk about that. Do we want Pastor Tim or Jaydon to officiate?"

He gave the matter some thought while the server came and took their orders.

Pastor Tim had been Well of Hope's senior pastor since they were in diapers. His son Jaydon used to be their youth pastor but had since transitioned into an associate pastor role.

"We know Jaydon better, but Pastor Tim is seasoned."

"Are we talking steaks or ceremonies?"

Conrad laughed. "Who would you prefer?"

Ashlyn's unfocused gaze wandered over the dining area for several long beats. Their server arrived with her fancy bacon and blue cheese patty melt and his open-faced green chile meatloaf sandwich. Smelled like heaven. Colorado might serve green chile, but it didn't hold a candle to New Mexico's.

He studied Ashlyn, anticipating she'd choose Jaydon, if only because the pastor and his wife, Gina, did premarital counseling together. Gina had experience with some of the trauma-related anxiety that still surfaced now and then in Ashlyn.

His stomach churned. Over twenty years after the fact, and he still felt sick when the memories hit.

"I love Pastor Tim and Mrs. Vivian, but I think I'd feel more comfortable counseling with Jaydon and Gina. There's more history there."

Conrad traced his thumb over her knuckles across the table surface, wishing he could turn back time and warn their families of the trouble they'd face on that fateful camping trip.

"I agree. We need to talk about a few other things too."

She glanced up at him with widened eyes. "Everything okay?"

"It's about Colorado."

Chapter Three

Worry broke out in gooseflesh along Ashlyn's arms. Her dinner smelled amazing, but she barely picked at a few of her sweet potato fries. She lifted the patty melt and forced herself to take a bite, knowing Conrad wouldn't let her get away with a few mere nibbles. After choking down the mouthful, she dusted the crumbs off and waved her fingers.

"Lay it on me, baby. Colorado." She aimed for light and goofy to banish the cloud of concern.

Conrad finished chewing before replying.

"They made an offer." He took another bite.

She stared. How could he eat while leaving her in such suspense? His gray-blue eyes gleamed with the smile his mouth was too full to make.

He swallowed and wiped his mouth on a napkin, glanced around, and leaned forward. She mirrored him, anticipation causing butterflies to dance in her belly. Shoving a fry into her mouth temporarily quieted them.

The next fry fell to her plate when Conrad named a significantly higher figure than he currently made. Her eyes bugged as he described the kind of flights they wanted him for, then the benefits and flexible schedule.

"That's your dream job, Con. Did you take it then and there?"

He shook his head. "Wanted to talk with you first."

Warmth swirled through her middle at his consideration of her input. One of a multitude of reasons she looked forward to marrying this man October 7.

From the look on his face, he had more to say. Too bad her mother chose that moment to call. Ashlyn hit Ignore and set her phone to silent. Conrad's blond eyebrow lifted.

"She's going to have to get used to boundaries once we're married, right? It's good practice."

He chuckled and leaned across the table. She gladly met him in the middle for a gentle touch of their lips. Didn't matter that she'd been kissing these lips close to half her life—she'd never tire of them.

His phone buzzed. Groaning, they dropped to their seats as he checked the screen. He sighed and handed her the phone.

"Everything okay, Mom?"

"I'm sorry to bother, but I need you. How soon can you be here?"

"What's the problem?" She'd venture the trouble wasn't an emergency by the loosest of standards.

"It's my computer. I was updating your wedding website, and it just disappeared . . ." her mother rambled on in great detail.

Ashlyn could probably help by phone, but it would take ten times longer. She ended the call with a groan and pushed her plate away.

"Gotta run?"

She grimaced with a nod. "I'm sorry."

"So much for boundaries," he said with a wry smile.

"Hey, I'm trying."

"I know." He did know, better than anyone. "Come on, then. I'll follow you. Tell me what's up while we walk out."

Conrad dropped a few bills on the table and tossed the waitress a wave as they stood to go.

An hour later, the pair sat at Mom's kitchen table, the nonemergency easily remedied, nibbling on freshly baked oatmeal chocolate chip cookies. Ashlyn's favorite, which meant Mom had something up her sleeve.

"I'm so sorry to interrupt your date. But since you're here, I have a few things to run by you."

Mom disappeared into her home office, or as they lovingly referred to it, *Command Central*. Aubrey Scott and her business partner, Lionel, owned Memorable Events, but she'd delegated most of the hands-on work to her underlings this year so she could focus on Ashlyn and Conrad's wedding. Her home office resembled something out of a behavioral analysis crime show, with its meticulously organized wall-to-wall dry erase boards and pegboards, swatch-covered table, and binder-filled desk.

Ashlyn glanced at Conrad, certain her brows were similarly tipped downward. What could the woman possibly add to the spectacle this wedding was sure to be? Ashlyn's ears perked at the sound of the sliding door to the office closet. Some rustling and a minute later, Mom reappeared with a garment bag.

Oh, good heavens. What now?

Conrad's hand slid into hers, soothing her nerves with a gentle squeeze. Come what may, he had her back. Besides, it didn't really matter. *This* wedding was for their mothers.

Expecting to see the garish atrocity of her mother's old wedding dress, Ashlyn's mouth dropped at the sight of a blush-pink bridesmaid's dress. Freed from the bag, the fabric shimmered in the hall light. Clean lines. Simple construction. The antithesis of everything her mother had chosen for the wedding to this point. If not for being the wrong color, Ashlyn would love it.

"Is this a sample dress?" A sinking feeling sagged her shoulders.

"No, it's Bianca's. Isn't it perfect?"

Ashlyn inhaled four long counts, held it for two, and released for three. She'd deliberately *not* asked her cousin to be in the wedding. The woman wanted Conrad for herself and refused to concede defeat despite his not-always-gentle rejections.

"It's lovely. But why . . .?"

"Oh, Miley's out. Bianca's in. And the bridesmaids will look so much better in pink. I've worked up new sample boards. Come see."

Miley couldn't make it? Why hadn't her former classmate called with the news herself? Ashlyn's eyes narrowed. More likely, this was another of her mother's machinations. She made a mental note to call her friend later and confirm.

Casting another worried glance at Conrad, Ashlyn took two hesitant steps into her mother's domain and sighed with dismay. Gone were the painstakingly assembled inspiration boards of burgundy, navy, and dusty blue—colors she actually liked—and one of the few aspects she'd chosen herself without being railroaded. In their place stood replicas in a whole new scheme of blush pink, sea glass, and cocoa powder. Fine colors for a spring or fall wedding, but they weren't *Ashlyn*.

She much preferred to balance bold jewel tones with pastel shades, a reflection of her faceted personality—the soft, docile daughter who cowed to her overbearing mother versus the strong, opinionated young woman who yearned for courage and adventure. Seeing the soft colors through that lens snapped something inside. Nothing would ever change unless she set change in motion herself.

"Mom," she began. *You can do this.* "I don't want Bianca, and I don't want these colors."

There. She'd stood up to her mother and survived.

Before her heart could leap with too much pride, Mom froze and gave her The Look.

Then *laughed*.

Ashlyn swallowed and studied her shoes.

"Darling, your colors were fine for a winter wedding. But you're getting married in October. These colors are much more fashionable. Trust me. This is what I do for a living. My expertise has kept you fed and sheltered since—"

Since Dad died. She didn't have to finish to drive the point home. Guilt swamped Ashlyn afresh. Would there ever come a day they could talk about Dad when she wouldn't feel this weight?

"You have impeccable taste, Mrs. Scott. But don't you think it's too close to the big day to switch the colors?"

God bless Conrad. She breathed in and out slowly and drew strength from the comfort of his hand in hers. He'd always been the brave one.

"Conrad's got a point, Mom. Everything has been planned around the colors for a year. We even have the invitations ready to mail this week."

13

Mom waved a dismissive hand. "Easily managed with a few calls. Now—"

"No, Mom," Ashlyn said more firmly this time. Conrad squeezed her fingers again, a silent encouragement. "I want the colors we had. And *no* Bianca."

Mom crossed her arms and gave them a shrewd look. A heartbeat before Ashlyn caved, Mom gave a quick nod. "I'll concede the colors, but Bianca stays. She's your cousin."

Disbelief and elation set off fireworks inside. A counteroffer she could live with. Conrad could introduce one of his pilot buddies to her cousin. Or maybe one of the search-and-rescue guys—they were pretty fit with all the training they had to do. Bianca wouldn't be able to resist. She hoped.

"Deal. Anything else?" She prayed her face matched the even tone she tried so hard to maintain. *Don't let her see you waffle!*

Give Aubrey Scott an inch, and she'd take a dozen miles.

"No. I was going to ask about centerpieces with the new color scheme, but since you've shot me down, the point is moot."

"Thanks, Mom." Ashlyn hugged her mother, whose expression softened with affection.

"You're welcome, sweetheart. Love you."

"Love you too. We're going to go hang out on the porch until Conrad has to head home."

"All right. Stop over at your mother's first." The Look aimed at Conrad this time. "She'll know you were here."

"Yes, ma'am."

Conrad held the front door for her, a habit Ashlyn adored.

"I'll text Mom later." He motioned to the house next door with his chin before flicking the switch on the bottom of an electric hurricane candle.

"Thank you." Ashlyn sagged to the front porch swing her father had hung twenty-something years ago, grateful Conrad never judged her fear of the dark.

"No place I'd rather be."

Conrad nudged his foot against the ground to set them in motion before stretching his arm across the top. The kiss he pressed behind her ear gave her the shivers.

She couldn't wait until they could afford a house with a porch swing like this. The dream was easy to picture. After all, she'd been

14

having it since Conrad had finally hit a growth spurt at fourteen, and she'd begun to see him differently.

Her lips twitched, recalling how awkward that year had been. In addition to the glasses she'd worn since fourth grade, she'd had to get braces. A lowly middle schooler, she didn't know how to act around her suddenly attractive best friend and his much cooler high school friends. But Conrad had been amazing even then. He didn't mind her hanging around, gawking and tongue-tied. Instead, he found ways to include her and make her feel special. Still did.

"They want me to report in three weeks."

Ashlyn sat ramrod straight.

"Three weeks?" she squeaked.

She caught his nod in the dim glow of the electric candle.

"September twelfth."

Her heart clenched so hard she thought it would implode. Barely a week before *the* anniversary. He wouldn't be able to come home so soon, which meant she'd have to observe it alone with her mother. After all they'd planned, after all she'd been trying to achieve before the big day—big *days*—

Her lungs seized.

"Hey." He ran his hand down her arm and pulled her close. "I'll be here the twenty-first, okay? I'll let them know I can't start until after that if they object."

She sucked in a desperate breath of air when her muscles eased enough for her lungs to cooperate again. Until she realized that no matter which week it happened, Conrad would still be moving without her.

Two days apart felt like an eternity. How would she survive weeks? The wedding wasn't until the first weekend of October. *Oh, no.* Would they still get a honeymoon?

"I already told them about the wedding and honeymoon."

Her muscles relaxed. Praise God Conrad could read and allay her fears before she had to speak them.

"C'mon. Let's pray before you tailspin."

The light teasing eased the corners of her lips upward. Being separated would test them both, but their love was strong enough. Wasn't it?

Ugh, she hated feeling weak and needy. *Dig deep, Ash. Come on!* One of these days, maybe she'd be stronger, braver.

He pulled her tighter into the circle of his arms until her head rested on his chest. She couldn't close her eyes outside in the dark, even in Conrad's arms with the hurricane lamp and solar lights dotting the night, so she let her gaze land on the flower bed edging the porch as he prayed for direction, peace, and courage for the two of them.

Did *he* need courage, or was that prayer just for her? Conrad was the bravest man she knew. He was going to rock this move to Colorado. A chance to fly helicopters for a company he believed in, using all the training he'd been doing since high school—this was his dream. Of course he'd thrive in it, with or without her.

She just hoped she had the courage to go too. And to handle him being gone so long.

Chapter Four

Conrad studied the wad of paper on the floor next to the wastebasket, waiting for their second premarital counseling session to officially begin. He shifted in the thinly cushioned chair and caught a glimpse of two more in the corner.

Jaydon stunk at trashketball. Conrad smothered a grin. Nice to have something to razz the other man about when he came back into the room. Conrad checked the time. The pastor had been gone over ten minutes now.

"How are you handling the moving preparations, Ashlyn?"

Conrad's heel bounced as he waited for Ashlyn to answer Gina. The way Ashlyn's tension increased as the countdown to his departure diminished worried him. Three weeks down to two now.

"I'm doing the best I can . . ." Ashlyn's voice trailed away.

She'd been retreating into her head recently, as she often did in times of stress the past twenty years. They should probably address that in one of these sessions.

"That's all anyone can ask for," Gina Bennett assured. "Did you find a place to live?"

"We're going to look this weekend," Conrad answered.

"Nice. Have you broken the news to your families?"

Ashlyn gave Gina a deer-in-the-headlights look.

Conrad swallowed.

"My dad knows," he answered. "We'll tell our moms at the annual Labor Day cookout after we get back from apartment hunting."

The women made small talk until Jaydon returned from wherever he'd been called away to the past few minutes.

The big man closed the door behind him. "Sorry about that. How are we doing?"

He dropped a kiss to his wife's mouth, then grinned at Ashlyn and Conrad as he took his seat in the chair across from them. Gina glowed from her husband's easy affection. It was like that for him and Ash too. They'd been together forever, and yet she made him feel like a ten-foot-tall marshmallow even after all this time.

Gina summarized her conversation with Ashlyn, mostly centered around the move and the wedding plans.

"Actually," Ashlyn fidgeted with the hem of her long shirt, "we should probably talk about the weddings."

"Weddings, plural?"

Jaydon scratched his thick, long beard and raised an eyebrow at Conrad, making him squirm in his chair like he'd done as a teenager battling inappropriate thoughts toward the brown-haired beauty in the chair beside him.

He felt just as guilty now for going along with Ashlyn's plan.

Conrad cleared his throat. "Uh, yeah. Ashlyn and I don't want a big fuss, but our mothers do. The minute we got engaged, they started planning like they'd been waiting twenty-five years for the opportunity."

Ashlyn snickered. "Truth."

Chuckles filled the room.

"It's going to be a circus. We wanted something that's just for us." Ashlyn practically bubbled over with excitement as she reached for his hand and squeezed.

"The morning of the big wedding, we want to have a small, private ceremony with just a handful of guests. At sunrise. Will you officiate both?"

Jaydon grinned. "Of course."

"The pictures will be stunning." Gina nodded. "A sunrise wedding during Balloon Fiesta—*wow*. Will you be on the ground or in the air?"

"The ground," they answered in unison.

A few years ago, Joe, a friend they often did chase crew for, invited them on a ride in his hot-air balloon. Conrad had loved the experience, not unlike the first time he'd flown in a helicopter. But Ashlyn had ended up in the bottom of the gondola with her arms around her legs, attempting not to hyperventilate, before Joe brought them back to solid ground.

Jaydon opened with a prayer, then he and Gina took turns leading the questions emailed to Conrad and Ashlyn earlier in the week. No surprise they knew more about each other's hopes, dreams, plans, and expectations than anyone.

"What is your greatest fear going into this marriage?"

Conrad swallowed, unprepared to answer. Relief and concern struck at the same time when he realized Jaydon posed the question to Ash. This hadn't been in their homework.

"That Conrad will get tired of me."

His head shot up. "What? Never gonna happen."

How could she even think such a fear, let alone voice it?

She ducked her head. Gina discreetly put a finger to her lips and then pointed to Ash. *Let her speak.*

Message received.

"I'm not brave like you are. I'm afraid of too many things. I can't even stand up to my own mother and fight for the wedding I want. Why *wouldn't* you get tired of me?"

Conrad's feet itched to pace, but his rear had turned to concrete in the chair. He looked in desperation from his former youth pastor to Gina and back.

Jaydon studied Ashlyn a long moment before hanging his clasped hands between his knees and nodding at Conrad. "Before offering assurances she might not be ready to receive, why don't we talk about the things she's afraid of."

The pastor's tone softened as his gaze returned to Ashlyn. "You comfortable with that?"

Conrad's heart lurched at her hesitant nod.

Didn't she know he'd do anything for her? Didn't she understand he'd built his entire life around developing the skills necessary to protect her from ever repeating the trauma she endured as a helpless little girl in the woods?

"Okay."

He detested the smallness in her tone. She was so much stronger and more capable than she saw herself. *Lord, how can I help her see?*

"We've talked about some of your past before," Gina coaxed. "Perhaps that's a good place to start. What happened when you were young that made you feel afraid?"

How much of the story did they know? Ashlyn rarely spoke of it. Maybe this was the right time and couple to confide in. With his impending move, he'd feel better knowing someone unrelated to them had her back.

His mom was a great lady, but like Ashlyn, she too easily let Aubrey Scott take the reins in their relationship. And Aubrey would drive Ashlyn crazy if the two of them were left alone together for too long.

"I was kind of a shy kid, but curious." Ashlyn began in a surprisingly steady voice. "And I loved being outdoors, especially in the mountains. So much so, for my fifth birthday, I asked to go camping one more time before it got too cold."

Conrad scooted his chair closer to Ashlyn's for when she needed him.

"The first day, we set up camp and went hiking. We made s'mores by the campfire, and I fell asleep in my dad's arms staring at the stars. In the morning, we hiked some more. The dads took Conrad exploring while our moms cooked lunch, or maybe it was dinner, I don't remember. They gave me a snack and put me down for a nap. I was so mad that *he* got to have fun while I had to sleep."

Gina laughed under her breath, and Conrad caught Jaydon smiling. Ashlyn's cheeks pinked, but she mirrored his adoring smile.

"Your families have always been close?" Jaydon glanced at Conrad.

He confirmed with a nod. "Ashlyn's parents moved into the house next door when she was a baby. My mom was ecstatic to have another young mom nearby. They became fast friends."

At Jaydon's nod, Ashlyn picked up the tale he knew she didn't want to tell but needed to.

"Mrs. Greer was fussing over the meal. I crawled out and saw Mom talking to a forest ranger—I remember his uniform—and headed toward her, but there was this butterfly. I thought it came

20

to play with me and be my friend. It was so big and pretty." Her gaze dropped to her lap. "I don't know how long I followed that butterfly. It must've been a while though."

Jaydon crossed the room to a mini-fridge in the corner. He returned with a bottle of water and handed one to Ashlyn. Conrad declined his unspoken offer with a quick headshake, but Ashlyn smiled gratefully and took several sips.

"Thank you. Anyway, I remember the butterfly landed on a bush with tiny purple flowers. I sat on the ground to watch as it flitted about, but I was so tired. The next thing I remember is waking up shivering."

Conrad hated the rest of this story. He knew it as well as she did, though from a different viewpoint.

"Along with the stranger-danger talk, Daddy always told us, 'If you get lost, stay where you are. Yell for help, but don't leave that spot. I will find you.' So I stayed. It got dark, and I heard scary noises, so I curled into a ball and hid. It was so cold. The cold, the dark, and the fear are what I remember most."

At her shiver, Conrad leaned over the arm of his chair and clutched her hand. If Jaydon's office had a couch instead of these stiff chairs, his arms could provide warmth and comfort.

"How long before they found you?"

Ashlyn peeled the label on her water bottle. "Ten hours."

Jaydon whistled and glanced at Conrad. "You want to catch us up from your end?"

Conrad cast a glance at Ashlyn. At her nod, he swallowed.

"We returned to camp and found the moms panic shouting Ashlyn's name over and over again. After a while, a ranger came out of the trees, shaking his head. While he called in help, Dad and Mr. Scott took off on their own. When search and rescue got there, the scene exploded with activity."

He'd never forget the mass of people with all their gear and dogs. They'd been so calm and in charge yet filled the place with an energy that ensnared him instantly.

"How old were you?"

"Seven."

Gina exhaled, shaking her head. "Poor baby, having to watch it all unfold. I bet even then you wanted to help."

He gave her a quick half-smile. "Yeah."

"I can't imagine what I'd do if Cady wandered off like that. Your parents must have been out of their minds with worry."

Jaydon patted his wife's leg and motioned for Conrad to continue.

"They put big lights up, made a plan, and it went from chaos to scary quiet for hours. We all thought they'd found her when someone on the radio said they found a blue hat."

At the others' looks of confusion, he explained. "Searchers establish codes to protect family who might overhear. Things went crazy again for a few moments, then a team nearby jogged off with a litter and ropes. Everything went quiet again until the radio crackled. Second blue hat, no contact."

Ashlyn sniffed and made a few breathy hiccupping noises. Conrad's heart ached. This was the hardest part of the story to tell, and he was glad Jaydon mercifully asked him to be the one to tell it. He closed his eyes and sucked in a fortifying breath.

"A little while later, someone approached my mom and Mrs. Scott. Seems our dads got turned around after dark. It was light when they left, so they had no flashlights or gear. They tumbled over a drop-off about a mile from camp. My dad landed on a ledge, broke his leg, and had some internal injuries. Mr. Scott missed the ledge and didn't make it."

"Oh, Ash." Gina wrapped Ashlyn in a fierce hug.

He'd prefer Ashlyn took comfort in his arms, but perhaps she needed another woman right now.

Jaydon dragged his fingers through his beard. "When did they find Ashlyn?"

"They called in a heli-extraction for my dad's injuries. Pilot caught a reflection and told the searchers where to look. One of the dogs found her around midnight, hypothermic."

To this day, he couldn't adequately describe the feeling of seeing her blanket-wrapped body in the arms of a SAR volunteer as they broke through the trees near the camp. He'd never forget hearing Mrs. Scott's sobs turn to wails as she scrambled to reach her semiconscious daughter.

She ripped Ashlyn right out of the rescuer's arms and hadn't let go of her baby since. Moving Ashlyn to Colorado might be a bigger feat than they were prepared to handle.

Chapter Five

"Before we head into savasana, come into a seated position for pranayama."

Ashlyn followed the yogi's soft instruction and lifted her face from Child's Pose on the floor, transitioning to an upright kneel. Eyes closed, she regulated her breathing to match the pace of the flow before easing flat onto her back with her limbs splayed.

As the tranquil-toned yoga instructor encouraged the class to rest and quiet their minds, Ashlyn turned to prayer.

Thank You, Father, for Conrad. For Aunt Wendy.

Thank You for my mom, though she makes me crazy.

Thank You for Jaydon and Gina.

Thank You for giving me the courage to share my story.

With each blessing counted, Ashlyn focused on her slow inhales and exhales, consciously relaxing her body. Some referred to savasana as the corpse pose, but that was morbid, and she didn't like calling it *resting angel* the way some Christian yogis did. Proper terms suited her para-librarian brain.

Focus, Ashlyn. Breathe and rest in the Lord.

After all, this was why she'd come tonight. Ordinarily, she attended the Christ-centered yoga class on Tuesdays, but a relaxing Hatha flow today was just what she needed after yesterday's counseling session.

I trust You, Lord.

I trust Your plans for our future.

I trust You with Conrad and with our wedding plans.

I give You control.

With each breath, Ashlyn's tension eased further.

Your will be done.

You are good.

She spent the remaining moments giving her heavenly Father glory and honor and praise.

"Thank you for sharing your practice today. Namaste."

Ashlyn opened her eyes at the instructor's soft-spoken dismissal, blinking as her vision adjusted to the light. She'd sleep well tonight, Lord willing. Rolling to her side and then knees, Ashlyn eased herself to her feet.

"I don't love the New Age mumbo jumbo of these classes, but they sure do calm a body," Aunt Wendy murmured beside her as they rolled their mats and retrieved their shoes and bags from the cubicles near the studio door.

"Exactly what I needed tonight." Ashlyn yawned and slid her rolled mat into the teal knitted bag her aunt had made as a birthday gift last year. "Thanks for coming with me."

"Rough day?"

"You could say that. Want to walk next door for a smoothie?"

Her aunt readily agreed. They ordered and took their drinks to a bistro table in the corner by the window.

"I'm glad you invited me to class, but it looks like you need more than yoga. Want to talk?"

Eyes closed, Ashlyn inhaled and exhaled to recenter herself and nodded.

"Conrad took the job in Colorado. He leaves in two weeks."

"Oh, hon. I thought you two weren't moving until after the wedding?"

"They want him to start right away."

Wendy sipped her tropical smoothie while Ashlyn drained her strawberry mango.

"How'd your mom take the news?"

"We haven't told her yet."

24

The look Wendy gave pricked at Ashlyn's overdeveloped sense of guilt.

"We will. On Monday."

"Why Monday?"

"Two birds, one stone. We're going this weekend to check out apartments. Made sense to wait for the Labor Day cookout and tell both our moms at the same time once we had everything sorted."

Wendy guffawed. The few other patrons inside the smoothie shop turned in their direction. Ashlyn flushed.

"Good luck, honey."

"Won't you be there?"

"Not this time. You two are old enough and mature enough to handle your mothers."

"You have such faith in us. I'm dreading it." Ashlyn pulled another sip from her straw and savored the sweet-tart flavor.

"That's not the only reason you needed an extra yoga class this week, is it?"

Aunt Wendy was far too perceptive. Ashlyn shook her head.

"We had our second premarital counseling session yesterday."

"How's that going?"

"Well, I think. The first one covered the homework Jaydon emailed beforehand. Easy stuff. Yesterday, not so much."

"I've never known you and Conrad to fight. What happened?"

She smiled at the older woman. "Oh, we've had plenty of tiffs over the years, but yesterday wasn't like that."

Ashlyn swallowed and let her gaze wander to the darkening sky through the shop window. "We talked about the camping trip."

Wendy's eyes filled with compassion. She set down her smoothie and covered Ashlyn's hand.

"I'm sure it's on your mind with the anniversary coming up."

A small nod from Ashlyn. "I can't believe it's been twenty years."

"Are you okay, honey?"

"I'm trying. Between the anniversary, Conrad moving, the wedding plans, Mom springing Bianca on me as a last-minute bridesmaid—"

Wendy snorted.

"Yeah. Mom keeps trying to change things on the wedding too. Same day she sprang Bianca on me, she tried to change the color scheme. Then on Monday, she brought up serving cupcakes instead of the four-tier cake she designed six months ago. Thank heaven the baker told her it was too late to change the order."

"Five weeks before the event?"

Ashlyn smirked. "I may have called the baker from the bathroom and warned her."

Wendy's loud bark of laughter drew all eyes to them once again. "Clever girl."

"I've had years to refine my subversive tactics."

"You do realize you're going to have to confront her directly one of these days."

"Not necessarily . . ." Ashlyn trailed off with a half-smile.

"I'm sorry, honey. Your dad was so easygoing. He wouldn't have wanted your mom to keep you on such a short leash. He'd have encouraged you to live your life out loud."

Ashlyn liked to think so, but her young memories weren't enough to form a solid picture of who her father had been. He'd passed away too long ago to trust anyone's version of what he would have wanted. It was all too easy for the living to speak for the dead based on their own agendas.

Unfortunately, Ashlyn would never know for herself.

The familiar guilt heated her body in a nauseating wave. She battled it down. *What happened is not your fault.*

"Mom means well. She's just," Ashlyn carefully considered her next words. "She's just overbearing. I think her need to control comes from the same place my fear of the dark does. That camping trip left its mark on us all in different ways."

"Excellent observation, Dr. Scott," Wendy smirked.

"At least we know my brief stint as a psych major was worthwhile." Ashlyn's lips curved up on one side. "Seriously, though. Trying to understand the *why* helps me have grace instead of resentment."

"Makes sense, and for what it's worth, I agree. So where are you and Conrad staying over the weekend?"

"With his dad. And before you ask, Conrad couch surfs, and I bunk with his sister when we visit."

"Good. You're grown adults who can make your own choices, but I'm glad those choices include sticking to your principles."

Ashlyn's face heated. She'd never admit aloud to her aunt the number of close calls they'd had over the years. Temptation was difficult for any couple in love, let alone one who'd been together as long as they had. It was by the grace of God and conscious effort they managed to conquer the flesh.

Thirty-seven days.

Perhaps it was another bit of grace they'd spend most of those coming days apart. Temptation was easier to fight when it wasn't right in your face.

Wendy snickered. "You're blushing." She flashed a knowing wink.

"Aunt Wendy!" Ashlyn hissed, fighting a smile.

"Please. I was young and in love once."

"Still not a topic I'm willing to discuss with my aunt." Even if her aunt was more like a friend than a secondary mother figure.

Conrad's ringtone sounded from her purse. Ashlyn felt her face flush again as she answered. *Silly girl.* It wasn't like he'd overheard their conversation or her thoughts.

"Hey, I made appointments with the rental company to look at those houses you liked online."

She loved how their conversations always began as if they'd never ended. Aunt Wendy motioned to the restroom and disappeared around the corner.

"Weren't they out of our price range?"

"They'll be a stretch, but we might be able to swing the blue one. We should at least look. Who knows, maybe the property manager will love us so much they'll cut a deal."

"Unlikely"—she laughed—"but I love your optimism."

His laugh joined hers. "Is that all you love?"

"Fishing for compliments, huh?"

"A guy's ego needs regular feeding, babe."

Another laugh bubbled out. "Ah, yes. How can I forget Gina's wise counsel?"

The pastoral couple loved to tease each other, but their jokes were rooted in truth and always good-natured.

"What are you up to tonight?"

"Sipping smoothies with Aunt Wendy after yoga class."

27

"On a Thursday?"

"Needed an extra boost after yesterday."

"Gotcha." His tone sobered. "You okay?"

"Better now. Looking forward to tomorrow."

"Me too. I'll pick you up at six?"

"Actually, Mindy agreed to close up so I can leave by four."

"Sweet. Meet you at your place by four-thirty then. Love you."

"Love you too."

Ashlyn tucked her phone back into her purse and yawned.

"Let's get out of here." Aunt Wendy had returned, and she tossed their empty cups into the trash. "You're about to keel over, and I need my beauty sleep."

With a hug, Ashlyn said good night to her aunt and waited until the reverse lights flashed white on Wendy's hatchback before pulling out of her space and heading the other way.

"Mom? I'm home," Ashlyn called out as she walked through the door and set her keys in the bowl.

"Hey, did you have a nice class?" Mom turned from the sink and dried her hands on a towel.

"I did."

"Hungry?"

"No thanks. I'm exhausted. Think I'll go straight to bed."

"Oh, okay."

Ashlyn paused midturn at the dejection in Mom's tone.

"Everything all right?"

"Yeah. Just had something to show you."

More wedding changes? Ashlyn shoved a fist into her sternum to settle the fight between dread and guilt in her belly.

"Let's see it."

"Are you sure?"

"Absolutely."

Her mother perked up and led the way to her office. Ashlyn yawned but followed, praying it wasn't anything too out there.

"I put these together today. What do you think?"

Two dozen small bouquets of silk flowers lined the countertop along the office wall.

"They're lovely, Mom. Who are they for?"

"Oh, these are your centerpieces."

"I thought we decided not to do flowers so guests could see each other and converse?"

What were they supposed to do with the two cases of mason-jar candles and other items Ashlyn had already paid for and lovingly wrapped in jute cord?

"I found these! Problem solved." Mom dug through a box and presented a twenty-four-inch-tall glass vase with a thin stem. Height-wise, they were fine, but surely her professional event-planner mother could see the style didn't mesh.

"We'll wrap the bottom few inches with tulle and add a narrow mesh ribbon with a bow in the dusty blue. Won't they be lovely?"

They'd be fine, but what was Mom's deal? Why was she suddenly introducing new things this late in the game?

Ashlyn swallowed a sigh. This change wouldn't hurt anyone.

"Those will look beautiful. Thank you."

"My pleasure, honey. It's going to be the most beautiful wedding I've ever put together."

Shame crested in a wave Ashlyn wasn't prepared to surf. How much would the sunrise ceremony hurt her mom? This event meant so much to her. Why couldn't she just go with the flow and not make a fuss?

Was this about having control?

If so, that made her just as bad as her mother.

Oh goodness. I'm becoming my mother.

Am I going to do this to my kids too?

No. The sunrise wedding was about far more than taking a stand and planning the ceremony she wanted on her own. It was about—

Ashlyn shoved the thoughts aside and pasted on a smile.

"I can't wait, Mom. And not just because I'm excited to finally marry Conrad. You've worked really hard on this."

What kind of daughter planned a second ceremony behind her mother's back? And she'd neglected to mention the weekend trip to her mother. She couldn't take much more guilt or shame today, or she'd end up with an ulcer by morning.

"I almost forgot. We're going up to Pueblo to visit Mr. Greer for the weekend, but we'll be back before the cookout Monday."

"Why? I mean, they'll be here next month for the wedding. Seems silly to go all that way. Or did Conrad wise up and decide not to invite that man and his—"

"Mom," Ashlyn cut her off with a warning.

Her mother gave The Look but wisely refrained from finishing her sentence.

"Does Marylin know?" She stalked back into the kitchen and retrieved a rag and spray bottle from under the sink.

"Yes, Mom. Just because their marriage ended doesn't mean she'd keep Conrad from a relationship with his father."

"That woman should have grown a spine years ago."

"Mom, *that woman* is your best friend. And it's been almost *eighteen* years."

Mom huffed and liberally sprayed the countertops.

"Anyway, we're leaving as soon as I get off work tomorrow."

"But you'll be back for the cookout?" She glanced at Ashlyn and resumed scrubbing the counter.

"Of course."

"Be safe," her mother said with a long-suffering sigh. "Call me when you get there so I'll sleep."

"Yes, ma'am."

Sleep sounded wonderful. Ashlyn just hoped this conversation wouldn't undo the calm she'd found earlier.

"By the way, your final dress fitting is next Friday morning."

She pictured the ivory heirloom gown her mother thought she was wearing, then considered confessing about the dream gown hanging in Wendy's closet.

There went her last shreds of peace.

Chapter Six

"You're nervous."

Conrad's gaze darted to Ashlyn, then returned to the blackness out the windshield broken by the glow of his headlights.

She knew him too well.

"You get this muscle tick right," she pushed a finger into the angle of his jaw, about an inch from his ear, "here."

He turned and pretended to chomp at her finger, relishing her giggly shriek.

"It's going to be okay, you know," she said a moment later. "And Marley is so excited to see you."

His eyebrow lifted. "You talked to my sister?"

Ashlyn shrugged like it was perfectly normal for her to have a relationship with the half sister he barely spoke to by text a few times a month.

"She's practically my sister too, you know."

She wasn't wrong. After all, Marley was fifteen and knew Ashlyn as well as she knew him—if not better—since they apparently spoke on the phone often.

"Do you talk to Topher too?"

"Sometimes."

How did he not know this about her? And why was he suddenly jealous of his fiancée having a relationship with his twelve-year-old half brother?

He knew why. Ashlyn had always wanted siblings, but her father had died before her parents had gotten around to giving her any. She also didn't haul around a truckload of resentment toward her father the way he did for his, so being a sister came easily. Unlike the way he had to work at being a brother—and a son.

If it weren't for his siblings, he might not have a relationship with the man at all, so perhaps he should be grateful Ashlyn made the effort. He loved Marley and Topher. They shouldn't suffer just because Conrad didn't know how to navigate a relationship with their dad.

"Your jaw is ticking again. Relax. This'll be a quick trip, but a good one. We'll find a place to live, and you'll get to spend some time with family you hardly see. Best of all, I'm right here to be your buffer." She gave him a sassy smirk.

His jaw relaxed into a micro-smile. "Praise God for that."

A half hour later, he parked his Bronco and stared at the well-lit house Dad had bought after the divorce almost eighteen years ago.

Conrad had spent part of every summer in Pueblo with his dad and stepmom from ages nine to seventeen. At that point, he'd been well on his way to a pilot's license, thanks to the charter high school he'd transferred to that focused on STEM and aviation. Visits since had been sporadic at best.

Was he ready to live this close to his father's family on a permanent basis? Probably not, though he did look forward to getting to know his siblings better before they grew up.

Ashlyn's comforting knee squeeze pulled him to the present. He gave her a tentative smile, knowing she'd see every ounce of hesitation he felt. Her hand lifted to the side of his face as her warm gaze spoke of reassurance and affection.

"Come on, flyboy. You can do this."

He nodded and leaned in to kiss her. Warm, familiar lips danced with his until a current of confidence surged through his veins. With Ashlyn at his side, he could conquer the world.

"I love you," he murmured as they broke apart.

"I love you more." A beam from the dome light bounced off her glasses as she opened her door and gave him a final glance. "Ready? I'm going in."

He sighed. "Where you go, I go."

Before they'd unloaded a single bag, the front door burst open, and his siblings appeared.

"You're here!"

Marley raced into Ashlyn's open arms. Conrad smiled and glanced to Topher, illuminated by the front porch light. Topher's nonplussed veneer wiped the smile from Conrad's mouth. He certainly had his work cut out for him with this relationship.

"Hey, bud. How was school today?"

Topher shrugged and stepped aside to let them pass.

"You made good time," called a gruff voice from the kitchen.

"Not too shabby," Conrad replied when Dad leaned his head into the hall.

"Making decaf. Should be ready after you're settled in."

"Thanks, Dad."

"Hey! You made it in one piece." His stepmother smiled and wrapped him and Ashlyn in hugs.

Heather's warmth and kind heart had made it difficult for Conrad not to like her, even as a heartbroken kid angry with his father for leaving. All these years later, he appreciated how she'd opened her home every summer and loved on him, attitude and all.

"Why don't you take your bags down the hall while Michael finishes the coffee?"

They didn't have much luggage for two nights, but Conrad still took his time with the task. Halfway down the hall, he peered into Topher's bedroom. He smiled at the similarities to when this room had been his summer home away from home. Instead of his old Tim Tebow and Peyton Manning posters, Topher had two snowboarders Conrad didn't recognize. He spotted the game system while backing out of the room. They might find common ground there first.

"I don't care if you bunk with me."

Topher's expression matched the words, but Conrad didn't miss the hopefulness in his tone.

"That's a great idea, bud." Ashlyn met Conrad's wide eyes with a wink and ruffled Toph's hair.

The boy dodged with a halfhearted groan. "Not cool."

She did the same to Conrad and received a similar response.

The guys made eye contact. At the twelve-year-old's grin, Conrad rushed Ashlyn, wrapped his arms around her waist, and held her squealing, giggling body while his brother mussed her hair.

Toph's laughter at Ashlyn's thoroughly disheveled hair and cockeyed glasses put a grin on Conrad's face. He was in for a huge payback, but it'd be worth it.

"Oh, it's on, boys. Just wait."

"What's on?" Marley popped her head in.

"Revenge when they least expect it," Ashlyn promised with a playful glare directed at the brothers.

Marley met Ashlyn's hand in a high-five. "Sweet."

Later that night, as he attempted to stretch out on the futon Topher used for gaming, listening to his little brother snore like their old man, he smiled to himself. He'd actually had a decent conversation with his dad once everyone else went to bed. The resentment he'd always struggled with felt lighter, and hope crept in to fill the space.

He dreaded telling his mom about this move, especially when she found out they'd be living near his dad's family. But he couldn't deny that this felt right. He'd never planned to take Ashlyn away from Albuquerque, yet they both wanted to spread their wings and figure out who they were apart from their families.

Cañon City was barely an hour away from Pueblo. A little over five from Albuquerque. Plus, his dream job with his dream girl by his side. If it all worked out, they'd find a sweet spot with both independence and a safety net.

Thank You, Lord, for providing a solution that meets our needs. Thank You for peace about it. Please help us find the right place to live at the right price tomorrow.

Chapter Seven

Ashlyn speared a fork into her chicken-apple-walnut salad, chewing in a hurry before Conrad returned with their drink refills. *Please, Lord, let the next house be the one.* Hope dwindled as she mentally reviewed the places they'd toured over the past thirty-six hours.

Yesterday had been a total bust. None of the in-budget and available rentals between Cañon City, Florence, or even Penrose had sparked that *home* feeling she'd been searching for. Now they were down to their final hours before the long drive home to Albuquerque.

Father, please prepare Mom's heart for the news even now. And please, please let the next house be the one. She sighed and scooped another bite. *Your will be done, of course.*

Conrad set her plastic cup filled with blackberry iced tea next to her nearly empty plate and remained standing beside the table. "About ready? Appointment's in fifteen minutes."

Ashlyn scraped the remnants into the corner of her plate and nodded as she scarfed down the last delicious bite. This place deserved a return visit after the move. She wiped her mouth on a napkin and picked up her purse in one hand, tea in the other, and followed Conrad outside.

"Are you sure you're okay having to commute?"

Conrad shrugged and held her door open. She climbed into the Bronco and waited for him to buckle himself into the driver's seat before clearing her throat dramatically.

He seemed to chew on his words before giving his answer. "I was kind of hoping we'd live closer to work, not quite so close to family. On our own, you know?"

Of course she did, but she countered, "The rent's a lot cheaper here in Pueblo, and there are more places available."

"Not that we've had much luck so far," he murmured.

"I have a good feeling about this next one."

"Let's hope you're right."

What was with his weird mood?

Ten minutes later, they pulled up to the curb in front of an adorable little white house with black trim and a small front lawn. She couldn't say whether it was a craftsman, bungalow, or ranch, but the hairs on the back of her neck stood to attention as a shiver crossed her shoulders and ran down her spine.

While the exterior revealed little more than a wood-sided, pitched-roof cube that had seen better days, the feeling she'd been waiting for nestled deep into her heart and stirred a frisson of anticipation in her belly. Ashlyn glanced at Conrad, wondering if he felt it too. He grinned and nodded as if reading her thoughts, which he likely had.

A thirty-something guy in khakis and a polo with the property management company's insignia strode down the two front steps as they slid out of the Bronco.

"You must be the Greers. I'm Arlen."

He led them up the walk, listing off the recent improvements the owner had done. Arlen opened the front door with a flourish and stepped inside. Ashlyn moved to follow, but Conrad stopped her with a heart-stopping smile. The next thing she knew, he'd swept her into his arms. Arlen paused his spiel to chuckle at her giggly shriek.

"Newlyweds?"

"Almost," Conrad answered, his eyes never leaving hers as he stepped through the doorway.

"You know how to sweep a girl off her feet," she said with a soft chortle. "But you can put me down now. I can't wait to see this house."

Though it was just a formality at this point. He felt it too. She could tell. Conrad hadn't carried her over the threshold at any of the other apartments, houses, or mobile homes they'd seen this weekend. The sparkling kitchen and bathrooms and wood-laminate flooring were simply icing on the cake.

"Appliances are on back order, but it'll be move-in ready the end of the month."

"Are you sure we can afford this?" she whispered after they'd finished exploring every room—not that there were many—and confirmed that it was perfect for their first shared home.

"Bit of a stretch, but yeah." He squeezed her fingers. "Can you feel it?"

She beamed. "Oh yeah. This is it."

Arlen's voice interrupted their sappy staring contest.

"The owner just listed this rental two days ago, but I can't imagine it'll be available much longer. As you can see, it's quite a steal."

"No need for the hard sell. We'll take it."

Conrad tugged her into his arms and stole her breath with a kiss. She didn't argue despite having an audience.

One step closer to making a home with the love of her life.

***

"Seems like you and your dad connected better this visit."

Ashlyn had waited thirty minutes to broach the subject, and she couldn't take the quiet anymore.

"Better than expected."

She swallowed a laugh. Literally *anything* would have been better than Conrad had expected. She'd come with him enough times to know things never went as badly as he imagined.

After filling out the paperwork and leaving their deposit on the rental, they'd returned to his dad's house and had a great time visiting with Michael, Heather, Marley, and Topher until it was time to hit the road.

Shifting in the passenger seat of Conrad's Bronco, she analyzed his profile. "What's going on with you? I thought the weekend went well."

Conrad laced their fingers together, brought the back of her hand to his mouth, and kissed it.

"It did."

"Then talk to me. What's got you in a funk?"

Several expressions flickered across his face as he watched the road ahead. She was grateful they had a few hours of daylight ahead so she could study the little nuances in his handsome face when he struggled with the words.

"It's everything. The visit, the new job and move, the anniversary, the wedding."

Her heart pounded. What wasn't he saying?

"Not all stress is negative, Ash. I can't wait to marry you." He squeezed her hand. "Just a lot all at once."

Her heart rate eased some. He was right. "At least we can cross housing off the list."

"True. Though I'm not looking forward to crashing on Topher's futon for three weeks."

"It'll be good for you. And him. You remember how hard it was being that age."

He nodded but kept his eyes on the road.

"No doubts?" he asked a few minutes later.

"None. In thirty-four days, I'm marrying my best friend before running away to the beach for a week. And in forty-one days, moving into a house that God Himself must have picked out because it couldn't be any more perfect for us. You?"

"Never. But ... are you sure you're okay moving so far from your mom and Wendy?"

He kept a neutral expression, but she didn't miss the rigidity in his posture or the way his Adam's apple bobbed. She watched him another moment, working on a relaxed countenance herself.

"It'll be hard, yes, but you're my family too. I'm ready."

He had no idea the steps she'd been taking to be ready, to prove just how much she loved this man and would sacrifice to be by his side in every high and low forevermore. Hopefully, she'd be brave enough to follow through with her plan.

Ashlyn removed her left hand from his grip, trailed her fingers up his shoulder, and toyed with his dark-blond hair. It was longer than he usually wore it, and though she loved the way his clean-cut hair contrasted against his stubbly face, being able to ruffle the length between her fingers gave her a pleasant thrill.

Conrad shivered and flashed her a cheeky grin. "If we weren't on a highway going seventy-five miles an hour, I'd pull over and kiss you right now."

She gave him a sassy grin right back with an added wink. "And I'd let you. Now watch the road and get us home safe so you can kiss me sufficiently later."

Ashlyn's heart beat a happy tempo as Conrad's shoulders relaxed beneath her touch. Considering how she picked up on every particle of tension he carried or shed, it did her good to see him release the extras he'd collected this weekend.

She wished there were more she could do for him. Wished he didn't have to leave next week. Or at least that she could go too. Too bad they couldn't just move the wedding up.

Except she had a few things to do before the big day.

Things that had absolutely nothing to do with flowers or cake or satin and everything to do with finding the courage to take this major leap ahead of them. Because while it was absolutely true that she couldn't wait to marry Conrad, and she was mostly ready to trade her old life for the new one they'd build together, she was still terrified of all the changes ahead.

"Should we go through the next set of questions for Tuesday's session with the Bennetts?" Ashlyn retrieved her phone and tapped the screen to pull up her email.

"Don't we need a plan for tomorrow first?"

Her hands dropped to her lap. "Right."

She'd never been comfortable carrying secrets. Getting one of them out in the open tomorrow would bring welcome relief. If only she didn't dread the fallout.

She pictured the gorgeous dress waiting in her closet at Aunt Wendy's house. Harmless subterfuge to give herself a taste of freedom now and then was one thing. Completely upending her mother's world was another. And what about Conrad's mother?

The two women had been so close for so many years, far more than mere neighbors. Aubrey might be the professional planner, but Marylin had put every bit as much of her heart and soul into the event. Marylin had been the one to instigate much of the matchmaking all those years ago. The one to encourage Ashlyn not to give up when Conrad hadn't made any moves. Probably had a hand in nudging him along too.

"We know how my mom will take the news. What about yours?"

Conrad worked his jaw a long moment before flicking a quick glance her direction. "Could go either way."

Her stomach churned. That was what she was afraid of.

He threaded their fingers together once more. "We're in this together. Where you go, I go, right?"

"Where you go, I go," she echoed. "So . . . we just break it to them gently?"

Her fingers warmed where his lips touched. "Probably for the best. Like a Band-Aid. Now, what's in our counseling homework this week?"

Chapter Eight

Conrad slid an arm around Ashlyn's shoulders and pulled her in close, pressing a kiss to her ear.

"Sure you're ready for this?"

She shivered at his whisper. He grinned and kissed the spot again, hoping to distract her from the tension visible in her taut shoulders.

"Now or never, right?"

His lips curved to match her nervous grin.

Hand in hand, they stepped into his mother's kitchen, where the two older women danced around each other in final preparations for the cookout. Friends and extended family would arrive shortly, and Conrad and Ashlyn had decided it best to let the cat out of the bag beforehand to minimize the likelihood of a blowup.

Now that the time had come, Conrad second-guessed their decision. Aubrey could be rather passive-aggressive when ruffled, and his mother tended to get weepy.

Nothing to it but to do it.

Conrad cleared his throat. "Mom? Mrs. Scott?"

The friends turned in tandem with similar curious looks. He glanced to Ashlyn, who nodded and squeezed his left hand. He thumbed toward the breakfast nook.

"I know you've got things to finish, but can we have a minute?"

"Sure, honey." Mom wiped her hands on a kitchen towel and made her way to the round table for four.

Mrs. Scott studied them with her sharp gaze before dipping her head and following his mother.

Conrad squeezed Ashlyn's hand under the table after taking their seats.

"There's no easy way to start this conversation," he began.

"Oh, Lord, you're pregnant." Ashlyn's mother groaned.

Mom gasped and shot him a disapproving glare he hadn't seen since his smart-mouthed teen years.

"No! Mom! Why would you think that?" Ashlyn protested.

Conrad swallowed, feeling as convicted about the truth as he would if the assumption were true.

Before Mrs. Scott rebutted, he lifted an assuring hand. "No, ma'am. You raised us well, and we've honored the Lord in our relationship." Even when it hadn't been easy. "Truth is, we're moving to Colorado."

Ripping the bandage off brought relief. The women's stunned silence, not so much.

"What do you mean, *moving to Colorado*?" Mom finally asked, her tone providing too few clues.

He met her gaze with as much apology as he could muster. "Got offered my dream job. I leave next week."

"What about the wedding?" Always with *the wedding*. Did Mrs. Scott think about anything else anymore?

"Proceeding as planned," Ashlyn promised. "We found a place this weekend—"

"I thought you were visiting *Michael* this weekend." Mrs. Scott spat his father's name as if the man had personally affronted her when he'd left her best friend eighteen years ago.

"I'm sorry, Mom. We wanted to make sure we had everything in place before we broke the news." Ashlyn placed a hand over Aubrey's forearm.

Mom pierced Conrad with a look that made him feel eight years old again. He hated disappointing her. Hated even more that her

42

eyes pooled with moisture the longer she looked at him. His gaze dropped to his lap, unable to maintain eye contact.

Nothing made him feel worse than making a woman he loved cry.

"I'll hate you being so far away, but we've known this was a possibility. I just wish you'd been honest with us sooner."

Conrad swallowed. Mom had always been the diplomatic one. Ashlyn released his hand and squeezed his knee under the table.

"You're adults, and as much as we'd love to keep you close to home, you've got to do what's best for your marriage."

His head whipped up. "Mom?"

Her eyes glistened, but she wore a half-smile brimming with love and understanding.

"Marylin, how can you say such a thing? What's best for their marriage is to stay right here with family!"

"Oh hush, Aubrey. You and Andrew left your parents behind to move here, and you were three years younger than Ashlyn when you did it."

Conrad watched the interchange in stunned silence.

"Yes, and I was Conrad's age when I became *a widow*," the other woman snapped.

This conversation was veering off track fast to a place Conrad didn't want to go. "Mrs. Scott, please understand."

"No! You can't take my daughter away from me!" She leaped from her seat and stormed to the kitchen, rummaging through cabinets and slamming doors as she worked.

Ashlyn flashed him a worried glance before following her mother into the kitchen, trepidation in each step. Conrad watched a moment longer before turning to Mom with a pleading look. She nodded, concern tipping her brows downward, and rose to her feet. At least one of their mothers understood and would support them.

He stood and wrapped her in a hug. "Thanks, Mom."

"It's about time Aubrey deals with her grief." She gave him a squeeze and a back pat. "It's been twenty years. She needs to let go. I'm just sorry it took me so long to cut the apron strings myself."

He chuckled and kissed his mother's cheek. "You cut them just fine. I've been living on my own for how many years?"

"Letting go is a mother's greatest struggle. I'm so proud of the man you've become, honey. Now, let's go talk Aubrey off the ledge before our guests arrive."

***

Conrad surveyed the crowded backyard, wondering where Ashlyn had disappeared to.

"Colorado, huh?"

Conrad glanced down at the owner of one sultry voice that had made him cringe since eighth grade. Bianca Clements reminded him of a hungry mountain lion, with the predatory gleam in her eyes and catlike movements. Over the years he'd learned to treat her like one too. He fought a smile, recalling an article he'd read on surviving a mountain lion attack.

Tip one, avoid escalation.

"Hello, Bianca. You look nice."

Batting her lashes, she gave a demure smile he wouldn't buy for two cents. "Thank you, Conny. You look pretty *nice* yourself."

He bit back a grimace. *Conny* was a fine name for somebody's lovable great-aunt, not so much for a twenty-seven-year-old helo pilot. Bianca sipped from a can of diet soda and flicked a stray droplet from her top lip with her tongue.

Tip two, don't run.

Conrad dipped a chip into the guacamole on his plate and scanned the yard for his fiancée. At the same time, Bianca continued her one-sided conversation, heavy on the double-entendre, gradually crowding his personal space with her lithe body.

Tip three, make yourself big and intimidating.

Retreating two steps to the trash to deposit his empty paper plate, Conrad squared his shoulders and turned to face the persistent woman.

"Have you seen Ashlyn?"

"I believe she ran next door for more cups." She ventured a step toward him. "Gives us a chance to catch up."

"Don't you have someone else to flirt with, Bianca?"

His tone came out too sharp, but this was the merry-go-round she insisted on riding despite his repeated refusals.

44

"Aw, but I love our sneaky banter." Her lower lip pursed into a pout belied by the gleam in her hazel-green eyes. "You're not married yet."

Tip four, throw things at it.

"Might as well be." He spotted one of his groomsmen—a friend from work Ashlyn had suggested he invite—and waved him over. "Hey, man, glad you could make it."

They clasped hands with a hearty backslap. Conrad's eyebrow lifted at the interested light in Elliot's eyes regarding the petite lioness standing too close for comfort. *Perfect.*

"Bianca, this is my friend, Elliot Walker. We work together. Elliot, Ashlyn's cousin, Bianca Clements."

"Nice to meet you, ma'am."

Bianca blinked. "I'm about fifteen years too young to be a ma'am."

"Force of habit." Elliot chuckled. "Would you mind showing a poor, starving man where the food table is?"

Conrad smothered a satisfied grin as Bianca accepted the invitation and led the former navy man away. Ashlyn's instincts were spot on. Those two were cut from the same cloth.

Thank heaven. He didn't have to apply tip five; *fight back.*

"Nicely done, flyboy." Ashlyn sidled up and hip-checked him.

He wrapped an arm around her waist and pulled her in for a deep kiss. She'd never have reason to doubt his faithfulness and desire for her as long as he had the power to prove it. They pulled apart a moment later, and he grinned at the pretty flush creeping up her neck as she ducked to check for an audience.

"Everyone's preoccupied," he murmured. "Besides, a month till our wedding, people expect to see some kissing."

Her shy grin swelled his chest with satisfaction. He spun her around, putting her back to his front while they people-watched. The annual Labor Day cookout was in full swing, and everyone appeared to be enjoying themselves.

"Are you going to miss these cookouts?"

Ashlyn shrugged. "We'll be back fairly often, won't we?"

"Most likely. No guarantees, though."

The crowd was filled with people from church as well as extended family from both his mother's side and hers. Knowing they weren't leaving their moms without loved ones nearby helped ease their consciences about the move.

"Your mom's reaction was unexpected."

He rested his cheek against Ashlyn's ear. "I know. I just hope she means it."

"You think she's putting on a brave front?"

He loosened his hold by a hair. "Maybe. It's been her M.O. since Dad left."

"She's so strong though."

"That's what she wants people to believe. She cried herself to sleep a lot when I was a kid."

"My mom too."

"Yeah, but yours was mourning."

"A broken heart is a broken heart, and grief is grief, whether the loss was by death or abandonment."

Conrad kissed the spot below her ear the way she liked. "How did you get so wise?"

She chuckled softly, leaning against him. "Experience and a plethora of psychology classes."

"Aren't you two the cutest?"

They turned to greet Grace, then her husband Joe, the friends whose hot-air balloon they crewed for periodically.

"Weather's supposed to cool off next week. Free to crew?"

Conrad shook his head. "Sorry, man. Ashlyn might be able to, but I'm moving to Colorado."

"Say it isn't so. I'm losing my favorite duo?"

"Looks like it. We just found out a couple weeks ago."

Ashlyn flashed the older couple an apologetic smile. "I'll call you this week. I'd love to crew between now and Fiesta."

"Sounds good. We'll miss you, buddy." Joe clapped Conrad's upper arm. "Grace'll be in touch, Ash."

Ashlyn nodded. "Fantastic."

The spark in her eyes gave him pause. He'd swear it was her up-to-something look, but he'd seen firsthand her fear of flying. What could she be up to involving Joe and Grace?

Chapter Nine

"You can do this. Nothing to it. Just a couple of rocks and some shrubs. One foot in front of the other."

All the positive self-talk in the world couldn't unfreeze Ashlyn's feet as her head tilted to take in the dizzying scale of the mountain before her. She needed Conrad.

"He's five and half hours away and won't be back for a whole week. You can and you *will* do this."

She closed her eyes and focused on her breathing, listening to the breeze through the desert along the foothills of the Sandia Mountains on her first day off in a week. It was a simple hiking trail, practically right in the middle of a residential neighborhood. Not even high enough elevation for tree cover.

This was supposed to be easy. All summer long, she and Conrad had been training to move her past the fear. With the twentieth anniversary rapidly approaching, Ashlyn desperately wanted to be able to venture into the woods without freaking out. She wanted to feel close to her dad again, to honor his memory by being adventurous.

Plus, how was she supposed to move to a mountain town in Colorado if she couldn't manage to venture two feet onto a safe, populated trail that more closely resembled rocky desert than actual mountain terrain?

Forget it. It wasn't safe for her to hike alone anyway.

Ashlyn turned back, muttering to herself in frustration. She tossed her lightweight daypack onto the front passenger seat of her Ford Focus.

Baby steps. Or better yet, baby wheels.

She could drive up the backside of the mountain and see how far she could get on her own. When she'd made the trip with Conrad last month, his loving encouragement got them all the way to the parking lot at the crest for the first time in years. Unable to exit the vehicle, she'd stared out the window at the treetops, unending expanse of blue sky, and distant peaks, trembling yet awed by the beauty of God's creation.

Though the mountains called to her spirit as they had since childhood, she had yet to defeat her fear of the woods and the jagged drop-offs that cropped up from every direction.

Could she make it to the top and get out of the car this time? She would certainly try.

Secured in the driver's seat, Ashlyn made the trek along Tramway Road to the eastbound I-40 onramp and followed the Sandia Crest Scenic Byway signs until trees surrounded her car on all sides.

Focus on the road. She drove up and up, the road curving and winding for a good ten minutes.

Her eyes lifted from the curving road just long enough to take in the ever-thickening tree line farther up the mountain.

Practicing controlled breathing, she reached for her reusable water bottle and took a long pull from the flip-up straw. The cool liquid eased the flush working its way up her body.

"Lord, I can't do this on my own," she prayed aloud. "Conrad's not here, but You are. I don't ever want to lose sight of that. You're always with me, my strength and my shield. I choose to trust You."

Hearing her own voice helped her feel less alone. In a way, it allowed her to imagine Jesus in the passenger seat instead of her backpack, carrying on a simple conversation like old friends.

"I need Your strength right now, Jesus. Your peace. With You, I can do all things, including defeat my fear. And we both know it's time I got braver. Help me be braver with You."

A strange feeling of calm settled in her heart as she prayed, eyes never leaving the road as it twisted and turned and inclined more steeply. She'd felt this same sensation before. When? The memory sat right at the edge of her consciousness, stubbornly refusing to come.

She cleared her head with a quick shake and blinked as the road curved into its final turn at the crest's parking area. After choosing a west-facing space, she focused once again on regulating her breathing as she took in the scenery.

To her right, a massive cluster of radio towers. Ahead, a ridge of rocks and wild grasses. A ramp leading to the railed overlook slightly left, and at her far left the Sandia Crest House. If memory served, there was a gift shop of some kind and restrooms.

Resolved not to overthink it, she opened the door, strode to the pay station, and took care of business. Four minutes later, she stood at the bottom of the ramp.

One foot in front of the other.

She glanced around at the handful of visitors. In the corner of the platform above, a small family huddled together. The mother carried an infant against her chest in some sort of fabric contraption wrapped like a shirt around her torso. She smiled while her husband took a quick photo and called out to a little girl no more than four, twirling in a clumsy pirouette.

Ashlyn's stomach clenched as the child twirled ever closer to the railing. The father scooped the girl into the air, eliciting a shriek of half protest, half glee, then settled her securely on his shoulders. Minus the baby, it could have been an out-of-body sort of flashback from twenty-plus years ago.

Her eyes never left the little family as they exited down the ramp on the far side of the platform and headed to the trailhead along the mountain ridge. As soon as they stepped foot onto the trail, the father put the girl back on solid ground, holding tightly to her hand. He leaned closer to speak. The girl nodded before staring wide-eyed over the outcropping of boulders merely a stone's throw from the ledge.

"Excuse us."

Ashlyn jolted at the voice behind her. An older couple in matching nylon jackets motioned toward the ramp. She obliged and stepped aside. Her gaze flicked to the trail, but the family had disappeared into the trees. She glanced up the platform at the elderly couple now standing at the overlook.

She could do this. Determination filled her with each step forward until she came to rest at the waist-high railing.

The calming sensation she'd had in the car moments before blossomed once again as she took in the view of the city far below. Looking out wasn't so bad. It wasn't until her eyes drifted downward to the craggy peaks that made the Sandias so beautiful from a distance and dangerous up close that she fought the urge to flee.

She closed her eyes. *Jesus, give me strength to last just a few more minutes.*

Conrad would be proud of her. She snapped several photos on her phone, stepping back from the rail in case her trembling hands lost their grip.

Voices to the right drew her attention. A group of teenagers laughed and teased as they picked their way across the rocks and into the trees just below the radio towers. She longed for the courage to follow them, to boldly make her way into the trees and hear the wind blowing through the pines as she breathed in the earthy scents kicked up on the breeze.

The scents, the sounds, the sky—those were the things she remembered fondly from her early childhood. Even that horrible night, shivering and petrified on the ground, she'd found peace.

That was it! The memory she'd been struggling to grasp earlier. In the darkness, alone except for the wildlife she sensed but couldn't see, she hadn't really been alone. She'd fallen asleep because a peace she'd never known before or since had quieted her fears as she laid there watching the stars and breathing in the mountain air.

Ashlyn gave one last look around before returning to her car to make the trek home. *Thank You for staying with me, Lord. You were there then. You are here now. I don't deserve Your love, but I feel Your arms around me all the same.*

She couldn't wait to tell Conrad.

Chapter Ten

Where was he? Surely he was on the way.

Conrad knew how big this day was for her. She'd gotten Rita to cover her at the library months ago so they could do this. He'd said he would be here, so why wasn't he?

Ashlyn shivered and turned from her lookout position at the bedroom window facing the street. Crossing to her closet, she retrieved her favorite zip hoodie and slipped it on, running her hands up and down her arms to speed the delivery of warmth.

In the week and a half since he'd moved, the clinging heat of summer had relinquished its dominance to autumn, and she couldn't seem to get warm despite the eighty-degree days. Returning to her post, she watched the still-green leaves on the giant fruitless mulberry flutter in the breeze. In a few weeks, they'd turn yellow and drop all at once.

Other trees in the neighborhood had already begun changing. Part of her wanted to love fall, a favorite season among her friends, but while she enjoyed a decent pumpkin spice latte now and then, the season didn't hold the same nostalgia for her. She much preferred the long, sunny days of summer.

The clock on her dresser read 8:19 a.m. If it weren't for the late-night text confirming his arrival, she'd worry about him being unconscious in a ditch somewhere.

Her daypack was ready to go—had been for days—filled with everything Conrad suggested after their many mini-trips this summer plus a little something extra she'd ordered online.

She needed this today, and not only because it was the twentieth anniversary of her father's death *and* her twenty-fifth birthday. The past eleven days without Conrad by her side had been a roller coaster.

Mom had hardly spoken to her since they'd announced the move. Mostly, she'd left random sticky notes on the fridge or bathroom mirror, reminding Ashlyn of wedding appointments or tasks to finalize, as if she didn't see the same notifications in their shared phone calendar.

Besides the fact her mom seemed to have completely forgotten it was her birthday, what hurt the most was that this should have been a day they faced together. Instead, Mom's text yesterday had blindsided her.

HEADING TO SANTA FE FOR THE PEREZ WEDDING. I'LL BE BACK SUNDAY.

No mention of either milestone. No apology.

Those first few years after losing Daddy, Mom had gone way overboard celebrating Ashlyn's birthday. So much so, Ashlyn had almost forgotten that the anniversary of her birth coincided with his death. As she'd grown older, Ashlyn had noticed the correlation between the size of her parties and the depth of her mother's grief.

For Mom to overlook both was completely out of character. Especially for milestone years when her mother tended to throw herself into planning lavish events despite Ashlyn's preference for simplicity. Even with the wedding superseding a birthday bash this year, Ashlyn had thought they'd at least have a somber dinner together. Something, anyway.

A flash of light through the window caught her attention. Conrad's Bronco parked against the curb. *Praise God. He made it.*

She practically sprinted to the front door and yanked it open, needing his arms around her more than her next breath.

"Happy birthday, beautiful."

A vase, filled with an enormous bouquet of the most stunning assortment of flowers she'd ever seen, covered her favorite face. Tears sprang to her eyes. Goodness, how she'd missed him.

"Oh, Conrad, they're gorgeous. Thank you."

She relieved him of the bouquet and held it to the side so she could better express her appreciation and welcome him home. Conrad wasted no time in cooperating.

His mouth captured hers and sent her heart racing in a hundred different directions. One moment stretched into two, then ten, until she wasn't sure how much longer she'd manage to stay upright.

Sufficiently drugged by his kisses, Ashlyn turned on wobbly legs and pulled him into the house.

"I'll just, um, set these on the counter, and we can head out."

"Sorry I'm late. The shop didn't open till eight, and I wanted to surprise you."

"You're forgiven."

She stepped back into his embrace and inhaled his familiar scent. Now that he was here, her world was right again.

"How are you?" He pressed a soft kiss to her temple.

"Better, now that you're home."

"I missed you so much." His confession brought a smile to her still-swollen lips.

"Me too. Eleven days felt like eleven hundred."

"Sixteen more, and we're golden."

"Praise God for that." Her smile faltered.

Conrad pulled back and frowned. "How are you really?"

Ashlyn told him about her mother's text, and his frown deepened. Even with nineteen hours to process the information, she didn't understand any better than he did.

"Should we call her?"

Ashlyn shook her head. "Not yet. Let's follow the plan and see how I feel later."

His eyes narrowed, but he agreed. She retrieved her pack from her bedroom. Conrad took it from her shoulder and tossed it into the back of the Bronco while she locked up.

She listened to him talk about work and adapting to daily life with his family as he drove the familiar road through the mountains. The usual hum of nerves built inside, but didn't consume her as it had so often this summer. Still, she found it difficult to make conversation the closer they came to the turnoff.

Conrad parked and rounded the rear of the SUV to get their packs while she sat frozen in place, eyes wide and heart thumping. He opened her door and eased her chin to face him. Compassion filled the gray-blue eyes she loved.

He removed her glasses and set them on the dashboard. Crossing her body, he pressed the latch on her seat belt and guided her out of the vehicle. His arms folded around her. She closed her eyes and buried her face in his chest, grateful he understood how difficult this was.

"I'm so proud of you."

Tears burned the backs of her eyelids. He'd said the same thing on the phone last week after she'd told him about conquering the crest.

"Father," he prayed, and her heart burst with affection. "We know You're with us today as we make this trek. It's not going to be easy, but You know how important this is to Ashlyn. You know how she longs to be courageous, to do the hard things. Guide us and protect us, and also be with Aubrey wherever she is today. Please grant them both Your perfect peace, strength, and comfort as only You can."

Conrad's simple prayer eased some of the tightness that had taken over her insides while they drove. She swiped under her eyes and reached back into the car for her glasses.

"Thank you. You always know just what to pray."

He hugged her again and brushed her lips once. Twice.

"Only because I know you better than I know myself. I love you, but God loves you more. And He's got this."

With a nod, she picked up her pack and slid it over both shoulders. "You're right. Let's go."

The pair picked their way through the dense underbrush. She trusted he knew where they were going. Over the next hour and a half, he regularly checked his handheld GPS unit, changing directions and guiding her over fallen trees until they came to a small clearing.

Nothing looked familiar, though her gut said otherwise.

"This is the campsite."

Ashlyn swallowed, a million butterflies inside reminding her of the one she'd followed twenty years ago.

"Do you know where to go from here?"

"Yeah." He inhaled deeply and exhaled hard, proof this was as tough for him as for her.

They continued into the trees for another half hour. Up and down. Ashlyn understood firsthand how easily their fathers had gotten turned around. If not for the bright sun shining overhead and Conrad's GPS, they'd be just as lost.

His feet stopped abruptly. She froze, feeling his body go rigid beside her. Fifty feet ahead of them, the ground dropped sharply. Her hand slid into his.

Give me bold feet, Jesus.

Slowly they approached the edge. The scenery was stunningly beautiful. Tall evergreens and blue sky surrounded them. After twenty years, nothing remained to tell the story of the tragedy that occurred here.

She found a sturdy boulder big enough for two and sat. His arm slid across her shoulders, and she closed her eyes, taking in the scents of dirt and pine and the man she loved. Neither spoke, knowing this moment of memorial was enough for now.

Chapter Eleven

They sat on the rock in each other's arms for the longest time. Conrad was content simply to be at Ashlyn's side, ready to provide whatever she needed.

While he wished he'd been there to see her overcome her fear at the crest, he thanked the Lord he was here now when it counted most. Early in the summer, when she'd first expressed her desire to do this, he'd had his doubts. But then she'd shown over and over with her progress just how capable she was. Witnessing her confidence grow, every stride she made toward becoming the bold woman he'd always known lived within, was an honor.

Ashlyn removed herself from his arms, stood, hefted her backpack from the dirt, and set it on her vacated seat. He noticed the slight tremble in her hands as she unzipped the pack and removed a bubble-wrapped package.

"I'll need your help choosing a spot and hammering it in." She gave him a wan smile. "I thought maybe if I planned this, I'd force myself to follow through and not chicken out."

Her hands steadied as she popped the tape that sealed the plastic and carefully unwrapped several layers to reveal a simple wrought iron cross with a spike at the bottom. A small white enameled plaque engraved with her father's name, birth, and death dates dangled from chains attached to the crossbeam.

No wonder her pack was heavier than it should've been.

"It's perfect," he said. "Hammer?"

She nodded and pulled one from her pack. He chuckled softly. This woman surprised him at every turn.

They selected a rocky spot near the edge and pounded it into the ground. Wiping dusty hands on their pant legs, they stood and threaded their fingers together as one.

"I miss you, Daddy. I wish I'd been able to know you. And," her voice broke along with Conrad's heart. "I'm sorry for wandering off."

"It wasn't your fault."

"I know that. Most of the time. Still, it's hard not to think he'd still be here if only I'd stayed in the tent and taken a nap like I was supposed to."

"Ash . . ."

She cut him off with a sniff. "It's okay. I've had enough therapy and taken enough classes to acknowledge the truth. It was a tragic accident, and I was just a curious little girl. He rushed out to find me because he loved me. He should have been more prepared, should have waited for the trained searchers. In my head, I know all of that."

"Your heart still says otherwise."

"Sometimes."

The ache in Conrad's chest eased when she allowed him to pull her flush against him. He pressed a kiss to the side of her head and sighed.

"He *did* love you. And not one of us believes you hold any blame. He'd be so proud of the way you remembered his words and stayed in a safe place until help came. He'd be proud of the woman you've become. Of how much you overcame to be here today."

"I hope so. I wish Mom would've come, though. It might've done her heart the good it's doing mine."

They'd tried. In May when Ashlyn first had the idea, they'd approached both of their mothers. Neither had been surprised when both women declined. Twenty years was a lifetime to Conrad and Ashlyn, but hardly a blink to Marylin and Aubrey.

"I'm sorry she hurt you." Angry too.

There was no excuse for Aubrey ditching her daughter by text, today of all days.

"She did, but I'll live. We just have to keep praying that she'll figure herself out, loving her just the way she is."

"You're far more gracious than I would be."

More gracious than he'd ever been. He'd held an eighteen-year grudge against his father for leaving. Now that he understood why the man left, he'd chosen to forgive and work on mending their relationship. Not that he could talk to Ash about their conversation, especially now. She already struggled with the guilt over her father's death. He wasn't so sure she could handle knowing that his own father's similar feelings had driven him away.

"I'm sorry, son. But I couldn't go on living next door to them day in, day out after I'd failed Andrew. I should've insisted we wait for search and rescue. He didn't deserve to die. Going on with my life, my family alive next door—I couldn't."

"We could've moved, Dad."

"Your mother wouldn't. We tried to make it work for a couple years, but I just—gave up. I'm," Dad choked, *"I'm sorry I let you both down."*

Their conversation a few weeks ago still burned in Conrad's ears. Everything in him screamed to tell Ashlyn about it. He never kept anything from her. But the last thing he wanted was for her to feel guilty about this too, and she would.

"You know something?"

Conrad turned to face her. She gazed out over the drop-off, a beautiful peace he'd not seen before lighting her features. Her warm brown eyes met his, and she smiled softly.

"I feel better."

"I can tell. You want to sit awhile longer or go?"

Ashlyn's head tilted and her eyes widened. Conrad followed her gaze to a large black-and-yellow butterfly. It came to rest on a nearby plant with two fading blossoms. Her hand crossed to his knee, which she squeezed as if sending a message. A moment later, the butterfly flitted away, and her grip eased.

"I don't believe it," she whispered.

Her breaths stuttered as she continued to stare after the butterfly. After several long blinks, she turned her gaze toward him.

"That type of swallowtail is really rare in these mountains, especially this late in September."

"Okay . . .?" That didn't explain her shortness of breath.

"That was the same type of butterfly I followed twenty years ago."

Conrad's shiver matched Ashlyn's. He grinned, chiding himself for letting something so silly feel this ominous, yet he couldn't ignore the strange coincidence.

"What do you think it means?"

"Probably nothing." She smiled again, eyes alight with joy. "But it feels a lot like coming full circle. Like I've been a scared little girl hiding in the bushes for twenty years, but not anymore."

Pride surged through him like a heat wave. He leaned down and kissed her. And *kissed* her.

Chapter Twelve

Enough was enough. The Bible promised God would never tempt a person beyond what they could bear, but Ashlyn was rapidly reaching the end of her ability to handle her mother with anything resembling a fruit of the spirit, let alone honor her.

Despite Mom's hyper-involvement and occasionally controlling tendencies all these years, they'd had a good relationship. Well, mostly, as long as Ashlyn didn't push back too hard. Still, they were close, and this canyon of silence between them hurt.

It didn't make any sense. Her mother's recent behavior went completely against the norm, and Ashlyn didn't know how to handle it.

She yawned and stretched her body into Warrior Two, wobbled too far, and almost fell to the mat. This wasn't helping. With a frustrated sigh, she gave up and flopped onto the bed, staring at the texture of her bedroom ceiling. What she wouldn't give for an afternoon nap to make up for her interrupted sleep the past several nights.

With only a week left until the wedding, they needed to move past this. She didn't want there to be tension between her and Mom any longer. It was a festering sore, affecting every part of her life. Just this morning, Rita had asked if she was able to finish out her last week at work. She hadn't known what to say, so Rita patted her on the arm and sent her to alphabetize the juvenile lit section until she had an answer.

Ashlyn's ears perked at the sound of Mom rattling around in the kitchen. Should she go in there and attempt to build a bridge? So far, her efforts to reconcile had been largely rebuffed.

Why was Mom making such an issue of this? Where they chose to live was her and Conrad's decision. What gave her mother the right to act like a pouting adolescent?

Closing her eyes, Ashlyn attempted to relax rather than give in to bitterness or anger, but no amount of deep breathing moved her into a halfway decent savasana. Her right foot kept wiggling from all the anxiety racing through her body. Every irritable passing thought only increased her foot's tempo.

If her mother only knew how Ashlyn had been tempted to stay at Aunt Wendy's until the wedding.

Ashlyn rolled to her side and popped to her feet. Clenching her fists by her side, she paced from her bedroom door to the window and back, muttering all the things she'd held back over the years. Things she'd never actually say because she loved and respected the woman enough not to, but *wow*, did it feel good to give herself free rein to think them and visualize the confrontation.

She paused midstride at the fragrance of cookies wafting under the door. *Oatmeal chocolate chip* cookies.

Mom only baked when she felt bad or had an agenda.

Ashlyn ripped open her bedroom door, prepared for a fight. She stomped into the kitchen to find it empty.

The still-warm oven had a plate of mouthwatering cookies on the cooktop and a note on the counter to the left of the stove. She picked up the pink square and registered the garage door closing. Peering through the window over the sink, she watched her mother drive away.

What in the world? Ashlyn glanced at the note.

CHOOSE PROGRAM—SEE DESK.

Program? *Please no more last-minute changes.* Blowing out a heavy exhale, Ashlyn made her way to Mom's office.

Goodness gracious, what had happened in here?

The usual chaos had been swept into neat piles. Mom had removed the sliding doors from the closet and added shelves, on which everything was now meticulously organized. A task Ashlyn had hounded her to do for years.

She turned to the corner once referred to as *The Leaning Tower of Wedd-isa*. Six large clear plastic bins now sat stacked inside one another, their contents neatly sorted on the long counter against the wall. *Wait*.

Those weren't the contents of Mom's bins. They were the contents of Ashlyn's, the ones she'd been hiding in the closet at Wendy's. The mason jars with the tops wrapped in jute cord. Previously empty, now filled with a thin layer of baby-blue sand and a burgundy candle, like the picture in her Pinterest board. In fact, *everything* was off her Pinterest boards. The secret ones.

Place cards. Favors. The guestbook.

Silk boutonnieres for the groomsmen and bouquets for the bridesmaids assembled with the flowers she'd bought on a whim, unable to resist the blend of colors and hoping she'd find the nerve to tell Mom she'd canceled the florist.

Even the small centerpiece bouquets her mother had made weeks ago had been reassembled to include the same flowers, the boring glass now wrapped to match the mason jars. They looked perfect.

Tears filled Ashlyn's vision.

She approached the counter and ran her fingers over a hand-lettered wood sign that read *Choose a seat, not a side. You are loved by both groom and bride*. Sprays of white anemone, burgundy ranunculus, dusty-blue hydrangea, and navy-blue peonies decorated the upper left and lower right corners, painted by a master hand. She'd been eyeing it online for months but never had the nerve to say so.

Ashlyn brushed away a tear, overwhelmed at the display. A watery laugh bubbled out. *Everything* she'd wanted, though on her mom's grander scale. A perfect harmony of both of their dreams for her and Conrad's wedding.

Her heart ached to call Mom, to thank her for this incredible gesture. Then she'd call Aunt Wendy and, right after chiding her for tattling, thank her for making this happen. No one else but

Conrad and Wendy knew the dreams of her heart, and Conrad wouldn't have spilled the beans.

"I wish you'd have told me what you truly wanted."

Heart pounding, she spun at her mother's voice. She hadn't heard her come home.

"Mom, I—"

"No, I get it." Her mother held her palm out. "You tried, but I railroaded you into what I thought was best." Mom's face looked pinched, but with what emotion Ashlyn couldn't quite decipher. "And I'm sorry."

"No, I—"

"Ashlyn Riley Scott, will you let me finish?"

She froze. The tone was the same one that always made her cave, but Mom's eyes sparkled. What was going on here?

"Come on. Let's go sit with some cookies and milk and have it out, shall we?"

Dumbfounded, Ashlyn followed her mom from the office to the kitchen and into the living room. She parked at one end of the couch, Mom at the other.

Mom dunked a cookie into her glass of milk. "I reacted horribly when you and Conrad announced your move. By the time I realized what I was doing, I didn't know how to undo it. So I talked to Wendy."

Ashlyn raised an eyebrow. Before today, she figured the sisters-in-law hadn't spoken much since Ashlyn had come of age.

"I was always jealous of how close the two of you were. *Are*. But if anyone could help me figure out how to make amends, well . . ." She cleared her throat. "Wendy didn't have much to say at first beyond giving me your Pinterest password and muttering *grand gesture*."

That explained how Mom had accessed her secret boards.

Mom shifted uncomfortably and set her empty glass on the coffee table. She made another throat-clearing noise, her foot tapping the same anxious rhythm Ashlyn's did. "Until I showed up on her porch after Lionel sent me home from the Perez wedding."

Ashlyn's head whipped up. "Wait. He sent you home from an event?"

The pair had been partners at Memorable Events for eons.

"He noticed I was barely keeping it together. I thought if I kept busy, I could ignore the . . ." Mom's gaze drifted, unfocused, across the room.

"Anniversary?"

"Yes." Head down, her mother picked a piece of fuzz off her lap. "Twenty years. I couldn't wrap my head around it. When you and Conrad brought up revisiting the site last May, I—well, it hit me I've been *stuck*. For twenty years. It was easy to excuse when you were young. I had a child to raise, needs to meet. Then you were in college. When the two of you got engaged, I threw myself into planning the perfect wedding, and it wasn't until Wendy poured an ice-cold bucket of truth over my head that I realized what I've been doing."

Ashlyn smothered a smile at the mental image. "Which was?"

"Distracting myself from my feelings rather than dealing with them."

Ashlyn's smile broke free. "You think?"

Mom gave her The Look. Rather than backpedal, Ashlyn tapped her newfound courage and pressed on.

"Makes sense. You couldn't deal with Dad's death, so you focused on me and on building your business. Years went by with little change to the status quo until we dropped the Colorado bombshell."

"Exactly. Wendy was livid with me for missing your birthday. I'm livid with myself. What kind of mother does that?"

"One who's hurting."

"No excuse. I owe you an apology for that and so many other things. That's why I hacked your Pinterest and exchanged all my wedding details for yours. While I pondered the right words to say, I went to work to *show* you instead."

With a shrug, Mom flopped against the couch cushions as if the conversation had drained the last dregs of her energy. Funny— Ashlyn had always pictured the woman with bottomless reserves, going on and on like that pink battery commercial rabbit.

"Thank you," Ashlyn managed to say past the rush hour of thoughts in her brain and snot ball in her throat. "I love you, Mom."

She rose and extended a hand to help her mom to her feet. Mom wobbled and fell into Ashlyn's open arms. A spot on her shoulder grew warm and damp as they held on tight.

"I love you muchly."

The phrase from her childhood brought a smile to Ashlyn's lips.

For the next several hours, they talked and remembered over refills of cookies and milk until mother and daughter groaned and rubbed their stomachs. Laughter and tears had both run dry.

"It's past my bedtime." Mom yawned.

"Stop yawning—" Ashlyn said with one of her own.

"Can't help it. Wait—" Another yawn. "Have one more wedding gift."

Ashlyn's brow furrowed, but she followed Mom down the hall. Hanging over her bedroom door was the white nylon dress bag. Her heart sank as she turned to face her mother and apologize.

"I didn't peek," Mom said. "Wendy tried to keep me from seeing it, but I know a wedding dress bag when I see one. I didn't know you wanted your own dress. When you were little, you used to admire mine so much, exactly the way I did when it belonged to my mother. I thought you wanted to wear it too. I should have asked rather than assume."

She couldn't let the apologies continue, no matter how good they did her heart.

"Mom, I'm sorry too. For not seeing past your hurt to the heart and telling you how I felt. To be honest, I didn't plan to buy a dress. I made an appointment at the boutique just to satisfy my curiosity. If I didn't find anything, I had a beautiful backup plan. But then I tried this one on"—she fingered the bag and flashed an apologetic smile—"and it's perfect."

"Then you'll wear it."

Ashlyn hesitated, but the moment felt right. "Want to see it?"

Tears filled Mom's eyes as she nodded. "Please."

Her heart leaped for joy despite her exhaustion. "Hang on. I want to do a reveal."

Ashlyn ran to the bathroom to rid her hands of cookie residue, raced back laughing with relief and glee, and closed the bedroom door. The gown slid over her head and into place beautifully. She managed to zip it up on her own and took in a cleansing breath before flinging open the door.

"Oh, Ash." Mom gasped. "It's—it's —*you*."

A smile blossomed from the sunlight in her chest. "And look," she thrust her hands into the sides, "it even has pockets!"

Mom shook her head with laughter. "Only you, sweetheart." She sobered. "Thank you for sharing it with me."

After the dress had been returned to the safety of its bag on the back of her bedroom door, Ashlyn hugged her mom one more time.

"I can't believe my little girl is all grown up and getting married in less than a week."

"Me either. I'm really sorry for keeping my wishes a secret, Mom. I should've been brave enough to come to you with the truth. No more secrets, okay?" She paused, prayed for strength, and affirmed her decision with a nod. "Well, one last secret. This one's a doozy, and even Conrad only knows half of it."

Ashlyn bounced on her heels, thrilled to finally be able to tell someone besides Joe, Grace, and Pastor Jaydon. After weeks of trying and failing, she finally felt like maybe she could really make it happen this time. It felt right. And once she told Mom, there was no going back.

"Well, go on already," Mom nudged.

She let it out in one big whoosh. "It involves a sunrise ceremony on the seventh and a hot-air balloon."

Chapter Thirteen

Conrad's hands were sweaty as he parked on the curb next to the park Ashlyn had chosen for their sunrise wedding.

Thank heaven she'd finally told her mom the truth. Surprises were fun, secrets not so much.

He squinted into the darkness, searching for familiar vehicles, but the park appeared empty. *Strange.*

Joe and Grace should've been here already. They'd agreed to unfurl their balloon here instead of at Balloon Fiesta Park so their photographer could capture their bridal images without thousands of strangers gathered around to gawk.

Opening the Bronco door, Conrad's gaze scanned the sky for the Dawn Patrol balloon. He checked his watch. Five forty-five. A little early. *No need to be nervous—it's only your wedding day. Ha!*

Just before six, a caravan of vehicles—including a truck pulling a familiar enclosed trailer—turned the corner.

His heart sped up. Everyone was here.

An emergency call the night before last had kept him too long in Colorado. Thank God they'd found the missing woman and her dog before hypothermia set in, but he was tired and beyond ready to see Ashlyn. Two weeks too long since he'd held her and kissed her sweet lips.

Though he'd hit the road the first possible second yesterday, it'd been too late to get home for the church rehearsal and dinner. Instead, he'd attended virtually by FaceTime with his phone in its perch on the dash while he drove, Topher proudly serving as stand-in. Good thing they didn't need to practice the casual sunrise ceremony.

"Glad to see you made it, son." Dad chuckled with a clap on the back. "We missed you last night."

"Yeah." He yawned. "Thanks for being here."

Praise the Lord there would be time for a nap and some coffee between this morning and the afternoon wedding. Preferably with his wife in his arms.

"You ready for this?" Dad thumbed toward the center of the grass to their left, where he could just make out Joe, Grace, and a few other familiar faces getting the balloon ready.

"Absolutely."

Dad patted his shoulder and chuckled again. "Good. Let's stand by the burners. I'm freezing out here, and you're supposed to wait by the balloon."

"Roger that." Conrad walked beside his father to where Joe was positioning the gondola. "Morning."

"Happy wedding day!" Grace popped up from the other side with a bright smile.

Conrad smiled, though his nerves kicked up.

He hugged his mother, then Aubrey, whose countenance shone like a beacon. Praise the Lord for working things out between Ash and his future mother-in-law. Must be going well.

Ten minutes later, he'd greeted the handful of other guests and stood in front of the inflated and tethered balloon beside Jaydon. After all this time, the moment they'd been waiting for was finally here. Hard to believe.

Yet there she was.

Conrad swallowed hard at the first glimpse of his bride. She must be freezing in that flowing white dress, but *wow*, did she look incredible. She strode toward him with a determination in her steps that set his heart on fire.

Three feet from the balloon, Conrad couldn't wait another second. He clenched and unclenched his hands and dashed toward her. The temptation to swing her into his arms and kiss the living daylights out of her was great, but he forced his feet to stop their forward momentum a split second before they collided. Taking both her hands in his, he leaned against her forehead and gave himself a second to get under control.

"You. Are. Breathtaking."

Her soft laugh freed his grin.

"And freezing," she added.

Aubrey stepped toward them and said in a stage whisper, "Get the pictures, then you can put on this coat." Conrad peered out the corner of his eye and saw a long white cloak like something from an elven movie set. Only Aubrey Scott.

More laughter joined theirs as the couple moved into position. The photographer took several shots, glanced eastward at the brightening Sandia Mountain horizon, adjusted the settings, and snapped a few more.

"Are we ready?" Joe asked.

At Ashlyn's nod, Conrad paused. She beamed brighter than the glow of the burner heating the envelope above them.

"Come on—let's go."

"Go? Where? I thought the whole point was to get married here at sunrise."

"Still is," she said, exhaling as if—

He looked from her to the balloon and back. *No way.*

"You don't have to—"

She cut him off with a hard peck on his lips. "Yes. We do. Because I love you. From this day forward, we are one. I'm braver with you, but not because of you." Her hands slid up the lapel of his navy-blue suit jacket. "I have courage because I have faith in you, you have faith in me, and our strength comes from Father God. So I can do this. I *want* to do this. And we'd better hurry up because I want to see the sun rise from the air when I promise to love, honor, and cherish you for the rest of my days."

Conrad marveled at the woman in front of him. He'd never seen her look more like her truest self than right now, and she was exquisite.

The pale-blue sky blazed with oranges and pinks between feathery white clouds as they exchanged vows twenty minutes later. Grace snapped photos while Joe kept them aloft. Wisps of long brown hair escaped Ashlyn's delicate side braid. Conrad tucked them behind one ear and cupped her face as Jaydon gave permission to kiss his bride.

Hundreds of balloons filled the sky around them as part of the annual festival, but Conrad didn't see a one. His eyes closed as he bent and captured her mouth, pouring every ounce of pride and awe he felt into the kiss.

"I love you, Mrs. Greer," he whispered against her lips when they finally broke apart.

The gondola's other occupants chuckled softly, but Conrad ignored them and held his bride instead. As Joe found a safe place to land, he and Ashlyn were content to stare out into the world beyond without fear.

Author's Note

Thank you for reading *Braver With You!* This novella is a slight departure from my normal Christian romance and Christian rom-coms, but when I prayed over writing it...this is what came out. Ha ha! It first appeared in October 2021's *USA Today* Bestselling *Save the Date: A Christian Romance Wedding Anthology* with several other leading Christian authors. BWY represented the month of October, and of course I absolutely had to set it during the Albuquerque International Balloon Fiesta.

If you've never had the opportunity to attend, I invite you to plan a trip to experience the beauty and wonder for yourself. You can also ooh and ahh at the incredible photography online.

I hope and pray you enjoyed Ashlyn and Conrad's story, and if you're a fan of my novels in the *Everyday Love* series, you likely recognized Gina and Jaydon from book two, *Whatever Comes Our Way*. High-strung Audrey and her business partner Lionel with their business *Memorable Events* originally appeared in my free subscriber-only novelette *Just Say Yes*. You can get your copy by signing up for my monthly (sometimes bimonthly) emails at www.jayceeweaver.com/newsletter.

Last but not least, if you enjoyed this book, please consider leaving a review on Amazon and/or Goodreads. Your ratings and reviews make a huge impact! Thank you again, and I hope you'll join my WeaverReaders community by email or on social media.

Be blessed and may the peace of Christ be with you always.

Jaycee